Skipping Christm.   t

by
Linzi Carlisle

I hope that this Christmas story welcomes you into its pages, that it makes you feel part of the family, and that it brings you companionship, happiness, and joy.
Happy Christmas.

Table of Contents
The Day before Christmas Eve   1
Christmas Eve   9
Christmas Day   27

The Day before Christmas Eve

'We're doing the right thing, aren't we? Mary Nugent looked across uncertainly at her husband.

'Oh, absolutely,' Archie nodded his head, 'No need for all that fuss and bother, putting up decorations only to have to take them down again, moving furniture around, getting the old tree out of the garage and fiddling with the lights which never work.'

'And all the tiring supermarket shopping, buying lots of fancy food with half of it going to waste, and so many people crowding in the shops, fighting over the last of the Brussels sprouts,' Mary picked up her tea cup, taking an appreciative sip as she looked around their neat and tidy, modest, living room, 'and all the mess to clean up afterwards.'

'And all that fuss about a turkey, which I'm not even that fond of, give me a decent roast chicken any day.'

'Besides, my heart's just not in it, if I'm honest, we've got no one to actually make a fuss for...'

'Now don't you go getting all sad and upset again,' Archie looked worriedly across at his wife.

'I won't, it's just silly I know, it's just... well, anyway, Susan's tied up with her new man. It's been hard for her since the divorce, she deserves a nice man in her life,' Mary smiled brightly, 'it'll be nice to meet him, I expect she'll introduce us to him soon, she probably wanted to be sure about everything and it's only been a few months. She'll give us a call soon, I'm sure, and we can hear all about her busy social life, they go to lots of parties apparently, all something to do with Trevor's job. It's no wonder she hasn't replied to many of my messages lately, but I am pleased she's enjoying herself, we want our children to be happy, that's what it's all about.'

'And the grandchildren are with their dad for Christmas, which is nice for them, they don't want to be hanging around with us old fogies, much more fun to be spending time with their step mum and their new family.' Archie looked up at his wife, 'You know what kids that age are like, busy on their phones and computers and the like, going to the pictures with their friends, and Matthew was never any good at replying to our messages, you know that.'

'Boys will be boys, although - do teenagers still go to the pictures these days? Michaela's very good at that photo thing on her phone, I believe, always going here and there with her friends, and spending hours taking her photos until they're just right. I'm not sure how it works, exactly, but I understand she has some kind of fan group, or something, so it's very important for her to keep at it. She was telling me all about it when we popped in to visit a few weeks ago, you remember, when I needed to use the bathroom but she was busy getting her photograph just right. Although why she has to take pictures looking into the bathroom mirror, I really don't know. Of course, as Susan said, we really should have called first, they had a lot going on and she was very insistent that we shouldn't stay and try and help, although the kitchen was in such a mess, it would have been no trouble.'

'I used to be keen on photography when I was a boy, of course it was different in those days, now they just whip their phone out and then press a few buttons and the photo looks completely different. All a bit of a cheat if you ask me. Funny old world,' Archie leaned back, having finished his tea, and looked out of the window. 'Wretched dark days and nights, hard to tell which is which.'

'I'll close the curtains,' standing up, Mary walked to the lounge window as a young woman walked by, passing under the glow of the streetlight, her arms hugging her body in the cold, her head down.

The movement of the curtains caught the woman's eye and she glanced up, seeing Mary at the window, and giving a small wave in return to Mary's.

'Poor thing, she looks freezing, and always on her own. She lives in one of the new flats, I believe. There, that's better,' turning round, Mary smiled appreciatively at their small, neat lounge, 'it feels cosier now, perhaps we should put the heater on, there's a real nip in the air tonight.'

'I expect Richard will let us know once they've settled in, their flight landed this morning, didn't it?' Archie checked his watch.

'Wasn't it yesterday morning when they landed? Yes, I'm sure of it, but you know what those holidays are like, all the travel, and then so much to sort out at the airport, and then they have to get to the hotel.'

'They'll have been worn out with it all, probably had an early night and only just got themselves unpacked and had a decent meal.'

'And they'll have wanted to explore a bit. I do hope the weather's nice for them, do them good to have a bit of sunshine. Maybe he tried to phone us but couldn't get through - remember the trouble we used to have when we tried to phone our parents on our trips to Spain?'

'That takes me back, trying to shove pesetas in the slot in the phone box, all of us crowded in, kids and all, everyone wanting to speak at once.' Archie paused, smiling at the memory, before continuing the original conversation. 'And Sandy will enjoy the rest, works hard keeping their house spick-and-span, lots to do in a house that size.'

Of course, they have a lady come in, but Richard said she only does the heavy stuff, poor Sandy has to do most of it. And she always looks so pretty, Richard said she has her hair done every week, imagine that, her nails too. He's very proud of her.'

'Says he's lucky she married him, young woman like that could have had the pick of the bunch, he said, but she set her sights on him, even gave up her secretarial job to become a housewife.'

'And the age gap doesn't seem to bother them. I should pop the oven on soon, the pie will need a good forty minutes.'

'What time's Helen coming?'

'Well,' Mary looked doubtful, 'I suggested seven o'clock, but you know what she's like with all her theatre friends.'

'Nice piece of your chicken pie and some mashed potato will do her the world of good, she always looks like she needs a good meal.'

Joan stifled a yawn as she checked her watch. Three more hours to go. She glanced across at her son as he sat perched on the stool behind the counter, his head in a book. 'Sure you don't want to go home, love?'

Nigel Brockley looked up, smiling at his mum, 'No, I'm alright, besides, I'm keeping you company, aren't I?'

'Well, if you call sitting there reading one of your books keeping me company, then yes, you are.' She tousled his hair, 'It's nice to have you here, but it's not much fun for you.'

They both looked up as the bell above the door chimed, accompanied by a rush of cold air as the door swung open, signalling a new customer. Joan smiled in welcome at the young woman. 'Let me know if you need any help.'

'Thanks,' Tracy Miller held her arms tightly around her chest as she walked along the aisles, stopping in front of the tins of petfood. Looking around, she realised that she should have picked up a basket.

'Take the customer a basket, won't you, Nige?'

'Oh, thanks,' Tracy kept one arm tightly around herself as she reached to take the basket.

'What's his name?' Nigel was smiling at the little face peering out from the top of Tracy's zipped jacket. 'Here, let me hold the basket for you.'

'He's not mine, I'm fostering him for the holidays. He hasn't even got a name, poor little thing.'

'Mum, come and see the puppy, he's really cute.'

'I'm not supposed to bring dogs in, it says on the door,' Tracy's face was anxious.

'That's okay, my mum won't mind. What food are you getting him?'

Joan joined the discussion, having exclaimed with delight over the puppy, 'Here, you'll want some tins of puppy food, as well as some biscuits. We've got chicken flavour or steak.'

With the puppy's food decisions made, Tracy apologetically turned her attention to her own meal requirements, hurriedly grabbing a microwave pasta meal from the fridge.

'Um, do you have an empty box at all? It's just, I need a bed for him...'

'Sure we do, in fact, we can do better than that. You live in the flats, don't you? I've seen you in here before.'

'Yes, number four.'

'Then we're neighbours, Nigel and I are in number ten, we must be just round the other side from you. I'm Joan, by the way, Joan Brockley.'

'Oh, Tracy, Tracy Miller.'

'Well, it's nice to meet you properly, Tracy, and your puppy. Now, here's what we'll do, Nigel will carry the bag for you so you can keep that little angel warm, and once you're safely inside he'll pop to ours and-' Joan turned to her son, 'you know that basket in my bedroom? The one with magazines in, it's just right for this little one, and there's that old throw laying over the back of the sofa, we never use it. Pop that in the basket and then you can take it round to Tracy's. Put your jacket on, love, it's cold out there.'

'Are you sure? I don't want to be a bother.'

'I'm more than sure, and it's about time Nigel went home. I'll bring pizza in when I'm done, love, how's that?'

Her spirits lifted, Joan waved the trio off with a smile, before walking into the small kitchenette at the back of the store and putting the kettle on.

'Pie smells good,' Archie sniffed the air, 'I'll lay the table, shall I? She's cutting it fine, typical Helen.'

'D'you think I should send her a message? But I don't want to be a nuisance, she'll tell me off for fussing. I'll just turn the oven down a bit, keep everything warm, she'll be here soon.'

'Didn't you say you were out for dinner tonight?' Alex threw back his glass of wine, shouting to be heard above the noise in the pub.

Helen Nugent's eyes widened momentarily, before she groaned, throwing her head back, 'My parents, I said I'd call in, what time is it?'

'Relax, darling, have another drink, it's only seven thirty, the night is young.'

'Seven thirty? I'm late, I'll have to drag myself there before the world comes to an end.'

'Oh, don't go, darling, we're all going on to Maxwell's,' Zara pouted, 'they've got a show tonight, we can have dinner there. You can go to your parents any old time. Besides, it's Christmas, we want to have fun.'

'Fun, fun, fun,' Alex chanted, banging the table, as the rest of the group joined in.

'Well, I suppose...'

'Champers, sweetie, oodles of lovely champers, and oysters, yummy. Rumour is George Clooney's in town.'

'George Clooney's not in town and you're a liar,' someone squealed.

Alex grinned, 'Maybe it was Brad Pitt, or was it some other, equally gorgeous, Hollywood hunk?'

'Besides,' Zara wheedled encouragingly, 'your parents will be busy with family if they're anything like mine, siblings and children everywhere...' she shuddered exaggeratedly, 'Christmas carols playing, or worse still, the radio on for their favourite programme, gaudy tinsel strung everywhere, oh, and don't forget the mince pies. Quite unbearable. Tell them you'll call in after Christmas, you can't possibly miss Alex's party tomorrow night, it's Christmas Eve, and you bought that fabulous dress...'

'And Christmas lunch is at Salvatore's, d'you know how hard it was to get a table?' Alex rolled his eyes dramatically. No, you're far too busy, darling, it's party season and we're going to party, it's what we do best, and remember, you have to be seen in all the right places, you never know when a stage producer is on the prowl.'

Laughing happily, Helen nodded, 'Alright, let's go to Maxwell's, I'll send my mum a message on the way. Who's calling a cab?'

Mary and Archie eyed Mary's phone as it gave a little ding. Picking it up, Mary clicked on the message from her daughter as her mind silently pleaded - please don't say you're not coming, your dad's so looking forward to seeing you, we both are. Disappointed, she put her phone down and looked across at her husband.

'She's not coming, is she?'

Shaking her head, Mary stood up and walked towards the kitchen, 'Something about an important party she'd forgotten about and she's very sorry and sends kisses.' She switched off the oven, removing her chicken pie and placing it to cool on the counter, before returning to the living room, where she removed the cutlery and placemats from the dinner table.

'You alright, love?' Archie saw his wife rub her eyes. 'She's young, thinks the world revolves around parties and her friends, you know what she's like, always been the same, wanting to be in the centre of things, lots of fun and laughter. And she's always saying it's important to be seen in the right places, all to do with how they find their next roles, although she doesn't seem to have been in anything for a while.'

Pausing on her way back to the kitchen, Mary considered Archie's words, 'She's thirty-eight years old, Archie, and I hate to say it but I sometimes feel that our daughter's world revolves around herself. Oh, it doesn't matter, no point in getting upset about it all, it's just, well look at this stupid great big pie I made. It used to be her favourite when she was younger. She probably wouldn't have wanted it anyway, I should know that she has to watch her figure all the time in case she suddenly lands a good role.'

'Tell you what,' Archie walked into the kitchen, where he took the cutlery from his wife and replaced it in the drawer, 'let the pie cool down, it can go in the fridge for now. How about I pop out and get us some fish and chips from Saltie's? We can watch a Morse, I've got a few recorded, how does that sound?'

3

'It sounds perfect, love, it'll take our minds off everything. I'll get trays ready then.'

With his coat buttoned up against the cold, Archie walked the short distance to the end of Holly Crescent, and Saltie's Chippy, opening the door and inhaling the appetising aromas of frying fish, chips, salt, and vinegar. He waited patiently behind the two people in front of him, glancing out of the window to see a man huddled in a bulky jacket staring intently through the window. The man reached into his pocket and brought out some coins, which he appeared to be counting, his face grey and drawn with cold in the light from the shop window. Pulled from his observations of the man, Archie turned to the counter, 'Oh, er, two haddock and chips, please.' He paused for a second, before making a decision, 'Tell you what, make that three, would you? Thanks.'

Not sure if the man would be pleased or insulted, Archie left the fish and chip shop with his bag of bundled up fish and chip meals and looked around, wondering where he'd gone. The hunched shape in the bus shelter had to be him, and he walked the short distance to it, clearing his throat awkwardly. 'Um, I, er, well, look, I saw you at the chippy. Let me start again, my name's Archie, I bought an extra meal by mistake and wondered if you fancied it, by any chance?'

'Surprised, the man looked up, a small smile forming, 'I never knew it was that difficult to get a fish and chips order right, but I'm glad you did,' his eyes twinkled in amusement and Archie let out a laugh of relief that the man wasn't insulted by his offer.

'I'm Jeff, Jeff Lipton,' he held out his hand and Archie shook it.

'Archie Nugent, live just along the road there, number nine. Well, there we are then, here's the fish and chips, it's got salt and vinegar on it, so...'

'Thanks,' Jeff took the proffered bundle from Archie, 'it's very kind of you, I haven't eaten all day actually, everything took longer than I expected and it turns out my friend, who I'm supposed to be staying with, isn't home yet so I'm waiting it out. This will go down a treat I can tell you that.'

'Pleased to be of help. Well, I'll leave you to it, you're sure your, er, friend, will be back? It's jolly cold out here.'

'Yeah, he won't let me down, old friends and all that. Shouldn't be too much longer. And I don't mind sitting here in the fresh air, makes a nice change to where I've come from. Prison,' he clarified, at Archie's quizzical expression, 'three months for criminal damage to property.' He rolled his eyes and shrugged his shoulders, 'Not sure why I just told you that, I'd planned on keeping it quiet, start again and all that, must be your kind face. And this,' he held up the still-wrapped fish and chips.

Surprised, Archie tried to keep his expression neutral. The man, Jeff, didn't look the type to be caught up in that sort of trouble, there must be more to it, but he didn't like to pry. 'Well, I'd better be getting back, this will be getting cold. Take care of yourself.'

'Thanks again, I appreciate it.'

Archie glanced back as he reached the other side of the road to see Jeff tucking into his fish and chips hungrily. His own stomach rumbled and he turned into his gate just as small drops of rain began to fall.

'I still don't get why we have to go to Dad's,' Michaela grumbled as she fastened her seatbelt, 'Louise doesn't even like us, and Curtis and Brianne are just babies. I can't believe you're dumping us with them for the whole of Christmas.' Michaela's voice had risen steadily as she'd been speaking and she now nudged her brother painfully in the ribs, 'It's not fair, say something, Matt, will you? Don't you even care?'

'What?' Matthew looked up, 'Oh, right, yeah, they're just babies, Mum, like Micky said,' he returned his attention to his phone.

'I do wish you wouldn't call Michaela Micky, Matthew,' Susan Chavers checked her rearview mirror as she reversed out of the driveway. She had just over an hour to drop the kids off and get back, have a quick shower and get ready for Trevor's work do. She just hoped the dress from last year still fitted, she'd gained more than a few pounds, which did nothing for her confidence levels, not when she was going to be surrounded by all the women from Trevor's work who looked like supermodels, especially Pam, whom he seemed altogether way too fond of. She forced a smile onto her face as she looked at her children in the mirror, 'You'll have a nice time, and it's not the whole of Christmas, it's just three nights, then Dad will drop you home on Boxing Day.

'Well, I'm going to be bored stiff,' Michaela threw herself back against the car seat, sighing loudly.

Turning off the engine, Susan hurried her children along, pulling their bags from the boot as she checked her watch again, 'Help me with these will you? And here's a bag of presents to go under the tree.' They walked up the path to the front door of the maisonette, where Susan banged loudly on the door. Really, Patrick could at least have been looking out for them, he knew they were coming.

'Can you get the door, Curtis?' Louise's voice reached them faintly through the mottled glass, followed by a shriek of laughter and the low growls of Patrick's voice. The door opened and a young boy's face peered round it.

'Hello, Curtis, how are you? Are you looking forward to Christmas?' Susan tried not to sound too impatient.

'Mum, it's Susan,' Curtis took another bite of his chocolate bar as he walked off into the small living room, from where the sounds of a cartoon could be heard playing on the television.

Patrick hurried down the stairs, pulling a tee shirt over his head, to stand in the narrow hallway in his bare feet, 'You're early, we weren't expecting you 'til later.'

'It's half past seven, how late did you think we'd be?'

A young woman in her early thirties stepped daintily down the stairs, wrapping a gown around herself, 'Hi, Susan, hi, kids, you're early.' She wrapped her arms around Patrick, smiling at Susan as her eyes raked down over her.

Was she smirking? 'We're not early,' trying to keep her irritation in check, Susan passed the bags over to her ex-husband, before giving her children a gentle nudge. 'I have to go, I'm going to be late.' She kissed each of them on the head, before turning to go. 'Have a nice Christmas, I'll call you on Christmas Day, alright? You'll drop them back Boxing Day morning, yes?'

Patrick rubbed his hands through his hair, 'Boxing Day? I thought they were going home on Christmas Day?'

Susan was already halfway down the path, 'Boxing Day, no arguments, bye kids.' Rain began to fall and she switched on her wipers as she drove back home, forcing herself to remain calm.

Archie and Mary finished off their fish and chips, pausing the episode of Morse they were watching, to take their plates out and put the kettle on. Walking back over to the lounge window, Archie pulled the curtain aside a little and peered out. The man, Jeff, had gone from the bus shelter so his friend must have got back. That was good, he thought, the rain was falling steadily now and it wouldn't be very pleasant out there.

As he went to drop the curtain back, a Tesco van pulled up at the house next door. 'Looks like the Hopes have got a grocery delivery. They certainly work late those fellows, lugging all those crates of shopping can't be much fun, and in the rain too. I expect Andrew and Dulcie have got family coming for Christmas, that's a fair lot of shopping going in there, looks like some booze, too.'

'Don't be so nosy,' Mary joined him at the window, taking a quick peek out, herself, before pulling the curtain closed. 'Dulcie's got a brother who lives in Scotland, maybe they're coming. I'm sure I saw a real tree in their window, it did look pretty, but can you imagine the mess?'

'That's why we're giving it all a miss this year, let's back to Morse. Did you check your phone again? Maybe we've missed a call from Richard?' Archie asked hopefully as he picked up the remote control.

Richard threw the bed covers back, sweating in the stifling heat of Thailand in December, before clambering out of bed and throwing the balcony door open. So much for a sea view, more like a building site with a glimpse of the sea to the left. He leaned on the railing, thinking back over the evening. Sandy had outdone herself last night. Not content with berating him about his useless choice of hotel, she'd offended the manager, made a horrendous fuss about having to sit on plastic chairs, sent her meal back for being undercooked, and proceeded to drink too much and cause a massive argument, which had been lapped up by their fellow diners.

She'd been expecting a luxury hotel, and he may have been more than a little frugal with the truth about where exactly he'd booked them into. And just as well that he had booked the cheap, all-inclusive package at The Phuket Plaza, he'd thought, after checking his credit card statement on his phone the night before. The disastrous evening hadn't been helped by his questions about just what exactly she'd spent so much money on for a five-day trip.

New luggage, she'd informed him angrily. There was nothing wrong with their old luggage, he'd replied. She'd had to buy new holiday clothes, new sandals, three bikinis. Three! Planning on wearing them all at the same time? he'd asked. Designer sunglasses, which had got scratched when she'd got into the taxi at home, necessitating the purchase of another, hugely expensive, pair at Heathrow. And to cap it all, there was a bill for the Harrington Spa and Hotel, which, she'd informed him sniffily, had been a much-needed spa day after all the stress of preparing for their trip.

Had she been there alone, he wondered? He wasn't stupid, he'd noticed the covert use of her mobile phone over the last couple of months, her extra time spent at the gym with her personal trainer, which cost a bomb, her new hairstyle. It was probably over, he conceded, looking down at his stomach as it protruded over his boxer shorts. She'd probably lined herself up a younger model. Suddenly he had an overwhelming urge to just leave her there, to return to England. Smiling grimly at the appealing idea, he turned and walked back inside, leaving the door open a little for some air. It was no surprise that the air conditioner wasn't working, but it would have been nice of they'd had a fridge, he thought, grabbing a bottle of tepid water and taking a thirsty gulp. Tiredly, he got back into bed, looking down at his perfect sleeping wife for a moment, before laying down and trying to sleep.

The oven was on when Joan Brockley walked inside and removed her coat, taking the pizza through to the small kitchenette. She was lucky with Nigel, he was such a good boy compared to so many his age. Removing the pizza from its box, she slid it into the oven, before leaning over the sofa and giving her son a hug. 'Thanks for putting the oven on, pizza will be about twenty minutes. I'm going to have a quick shower. How was the puppy?'

Nigel's face broke into a smile, 'I'm taking him for a walk tomorrow, just a short one. He loved his bed, kept wagging his tail and rolling around in the blanket. Oh, and he liked the biscuits. Mum, he really needs a home, Tracy can't keep him because she's out at work all day, and...'

'And because she lives in the flat, like we do, love.' Joan tousled his hair, 'I wish we could, I really do, but you know we're not allowed pets here. Perhaps if we move to a house one day...'

'Yeah, I know. It's okay, Mum. Oh, and Tracy works at the library, she said they've got a sale on tomorrow and I can get some cheap books. I thought I'd go along and have a look.'

'That's great, I'll give you some money.'

'You don't need to do that, I've got enough.'

'It's Christmas, I think I can find a few extra pounds for my boy. Right, watch that pizza for me, I'm off to shower.'

'That's the last of it,' Andrew Hope handed his wife the pack of sausages in blankets, together with the pack of sausage rolls, 'looks like we've got enough to feed an army here.'

Dulcie squeezed the last items into the fridge and closed the door, standing back to survey the boxes of wine and bottles of sherry and whisky on the counter. 'You know how Alasdair and Gwyneth like their food.'

'And their drink,' Andrew grinned, 'it'll be good to see them, what time are they arriving?'

'They're catching the train in the morning, Gwyneth said they should be in London by mid-afternoon. Now, where are we going to put all these nuts and savoury biscuits?'

With everything put away, Andrew suggested a sherry, and the couple sank gratefully into their armchairs. 'It's very quiet next door, no sign of any decorations, perhaps Mary and Archie are going out for Christmas this year, off to one of the children,' Dulcie pondered, her eyes attracted to the sparkling lights on the small tree in front of the window. 'I still don't know what possessed you to buy a tree, but it does look nice.'

Tracy Miller hugged the little puppy close, burying her nose in its soft fur, 'I wish I could keep you.' The puppy turned its head up, its pink tongue shooting out at lightning speed to lick her face, causing her to laugh. The microwave pinged and, gently placing the puppy on the sofa, she stood up to fetch her dinner, peeling off the cellophane and grabbing a fork, before settling herself back on the sofa. She smiled down at the puppy as it dozed off, picking up her book and opening it at her bookmark.

Susan dragged a comb through her wet hair as she stared despondently at her underwear clad body. Reaching for her dress she pulled it on over her head, attempted to smooth it down over her stomach, and reached for the zip as her phone rang.

'Hi, Suze,' Trevor's voice was loud above the background sounds of music and laughter, 'bit of a hiccup here, you know what it's like, the drinks are flowing and the boys wouldn't take no for an answer. Are you alright getting a taxi?' Muffled sounds of Trevor's laughter reached her ears, a woman's voice, the music getting louder, 'Suze, are you there?'

'Yes, I'm here,' trying to keep her voice bright, she stared forlornly at her reflection, her hair stuck to her forehead, her dress sagging uselessly as it refused to be zipped up. 'I'll see you soon, okay? How's the party?' The phone went dead and she realised he'd ended the call. Opening her wardrobe she considered her options – there were the black trousers, they did fit, just about, but it meant she'd be uncomfortable all evening, especially if she was sitting down a lot. She couldn't, she just couldn't wear the dress she'd worn to Richard and Sandy's wedding, she looked like a flowery tablecloth in it, hadn't even realised how awful it had looked until she'd seen the photos, plus it was a summer dress and she'd have to wear the summery sandals with it and, seeing as it was now pouring with rain, that would be a mistake.

Checking her watch again, she made a decision, it would have to be the black trousers and a loose blouse to hide the straining waistline, it wouldn't look too bad with her black heeled boots.

Once her hair was dry, she stood back and appraised herself in the mirror. Not too bad. Grabbing her makeup bag, she hurriedly applied foundation, powder, and lipstick, before ordering an uber. With a quick spritz of perfume she rushed down the stairs and hovered by the front door waiting for the hoot of the taxi.

'Archie, what is it? You've been back at that window twice.'

'Just checking the weather, it's cats and dogs out there now.' Archie let the curtain fall. At least there was no sign of him, he must be alright. Strange how he'd felt concerned about the chap, something about his face he supposed, he had one of those nice faces. Funny that he'd been in prison, he just didn't look the type, that's if there was a type...

Jeff Lipton stood huddled up against the wind and rain beneath the canopy outside the convenience store. He'd ventured back to the bus shelter earlier but had seen the chap, Archie, looking out of his window, clearly wondering about him. He'd hang around a bit longer then try Russell's one last time, but something told him his old mate wasn't going to be in. The flat had looked closed up, curtains pulled, no lights on. Of course, he could just be out somewhere, it was the night before Christmas Eve. Maybe he was at the pub, he thought suddenly, feeling brighter, that would be it. There must be a local around here somewhere, although he had no idea where and it would mean more walking in the rain. Still, it was worth a try. He set off, taking a chance on the street to his left.

With relief, he saw the familiar pub sign and the light shining out from the windows, and pulled the door of The Bricklayer's Arms open, basking in the warmth that enveloped him as he stepped inside. The gents was on his left and he pushed the door open, using the facilities and, after washing his hands, blasted the hot air drier to warm himself up. Making his way through the crowd of drinkers, he stood at the bar, smiling at the barmaid as she walked towards him.

'What can I get you, love?'

'Nothing to drink thanks, I'm just trying to find my mate, Russell, he lives down the road. Russell Cronin? I think this is his local.'

'Sorry, love, don't know him, hold on. Den! Know anyone by the name of Russell from round here? Russell- what was it?' she looked back at Jeff as the man she'd called Den walked up to them.

'Cronin, Russell Cronin, he lives at the end of Holly Crescent in one of the flats?'

Den shook his head slowly, 'Russell Cronin... oh, you mean old Russ, hang on a sec. Oi, Franco, get yourself over 'ere.' His voice bellowed out above the noise and a ruddy-faced man in a Santa hat looked up, slapping the behind of the woman he unceremoniously removed from his lap. Picking up his glass of lager, he pushed his way to them.

'This man's looking for old Russ, know where he moved to?'

'Moved?' the word was out before he could stop it, dismay written over his face.

'Went back to Bristol, I heard, bust up with the missus,' Franco shook his head sadly, 'his own fault, got caught playing around, silly fool. She was a looker alright, his missus, I mean, not the little bit he was playing around with. So she threw him out, must have been about a week ago, then she only went chasing off after him. Sorry, mate. Get you a pint?'

Shaking his head, Jeff thanked him, declining the drink, knowing that he wouldn't be able to repay the gesture. Disconsolately turning to go, he nodded his thanks at the barmaid, who was watching him sympathetically.

'Here,' she handed him a glass with a generous measure of amber liquid in it, 'have a whisky, warm yourself up, it's on the house.' She winked kindly at him as he thanked her and downed the drink, warmth spreading through his chilled body.

Leaving the pub, Jeff walked slowly back along the street as the rain soaked into his jacket. Well, that was that then, he was officially homeless on the night before Christmas Eve, and might as well be penniless for all the good the seventy-five pence in his pocket did him. He passed number nine Holly Crescent, noting the dark downstairs windows and the light shining from upstairs. Reaching the bus shelter, he laid himself out along the seats, put his bag underneath his head, wrapped his arms tightly around his body, and closed his eyes wearily.

Linzi Carlisle

Susan thanked the driver, stepping from the taxi just as a fresh burst of rain fell, and rushed inside Trevor's office building, following the sounds of music up the stairs and along the passage. Seeing a sign for the ladies to her right, she opened the door in relief, stopping at the mirror above the basins to look at her appearance in dismay. Panda eyes stared back at her and she grabbed some toilet paper, rubbing furiously at the streaks of mascara as the door opened and two women walked in, bringing the sounds of the pounding eighties music with them, together with the slight smell of sweat beneath their perfume. They glanced disinterestedly at Susan as they carried on chatting, smoothing their dresses over their slim bodies and rearranging their already perfect hair in the mirror.

Once they'd left, Susan stuck her head under the hand drier in an attempt to dry her hair and give it back a bit of body. With a last resolute look in the mirror, she squared her shoulders and walked into the party, her eyes scanning the room for Trevor.

'Nice lazy day tomorrow,' Archie pulled his wife close and hugged her as they pulled the duvet up.

'No rushing around in the crowds panic buying...' Mary murmured as she laid down, feeling sleepy. For a fleeting moment she wondered again if they were doing the right thing in giving Christmas a miss, it did all feel a bit empty... and the house did look a little bare, with no decorations... she hoped they wouldn't feel too lonely...

8

Christmas Eve

Joan opened up the shop, switching lights on in the gloom of early morning. She hung her coat in the small kitchenette, switched the kettle on and tuned the radio to some cheery Christmas music, before turning her attention to the fridges to check the dates. Picking up everything that was due to expire the next day, she moved it to the front fridge where a sign declared that everything was one pound only. There would be the last-minute convenience shoppers, although most people would have bought all their food by now and would be unlikely to want microwave meals for one, or pies.

She turned her attention to the boxes of Christmas crackers, marking them as half price and, hearing the kettle switch off, made herself a cup of tea, nursing it at the till as she thought longingly of tomorrow and a day off. It wouldn't be much fun for Nigel, just the two of them again, and they wouldn't be having a lavish roast dinner like most people. With a shock she realised that she hadn't got anything special in for their meal. She had the grand sum of twenty pounds in her purse, having left a tenner for Nigel, with a note telling him to buy some books from the library with it.

Leaving her counter, Joan picked up a box of Christmas crackers and some packets of crisps and peanuts, taking them to the kitchenette, adding up the cost with her discount, in her head. She might own the small store, thanks to the modest life insurance policy which had paid out after her husband's death, but she held herself to a strict standard, never taking an item without paying for it. If there were some sausages and bacon left at the end of the day, she'd take some at half price, they could have a big fry-up for brunch, that would be a treat, she had plenty of eggs and some baked beans at home. And if there were some lasagnes left over, she could get a couple of those, pop them in a bigger dish with some extra cheese, maybe get a garlic bread to go with it... She found herself humming along to George Michael, it would be alright, she thought, not like the old days, when they'd been a family of three, but alright.

Looking up as the bell above the door dinged, she took in the man's dishevelled appearance and stubble, 'Morning,' smiling, Joan kept a discreet eye on him as he wandered down the aisle.

Jeff walked slowly, grateful to be inside after his night in the bus shelter, browsing the shelves as he checked prices, wondering what he could get for seventy-five pence. Not much, was the answer, clear and simple. He walked back up and found himself at a discount display announcing that everything was one pound. A quid, that was all, and he still couldn't afford anything. Surreptitiously he checked the coins from his pocket again, unknowingly observed by Joan in the mirror.

Poor man, he was obviously homeless and hungry and just wanted to get something to eat. He was obviously freezing cold too, would probably appreciate a cup of hot tea, and she had just boiled the kettle...

'I was just about to mark those sausage rolls down to twenty-five pence,' she walked out from behind the counter, 'and we've got a microwave to heat them up for you if you want. And, because it's Christmas, I'm offering all my customers a cuppa, can I make you one, the kettle's just boiled?'

Jeff gratefully accepted the cup of tea from Joan as he ate the hot sausage roll, warmth and energy returning to his bones. 'This was just what I needed, thank you, it's very kind of you.'

'No problem, it's taters out there, you must be freezing,' Joan subtly studied the man's face - it was a kind face, and he spoke nicely – she wondered what circumstances had brought him to his current situation. 'I'll leave you to finish your other sausage roll and your tea, and no rush, take your time, I don't mind a bit of company in the shop.' She gave him some space, busying herself at the till and popping in the extra cash for the sausage rolls she'd reduced for him.

'You're at that window again, Archie, something's bothering you, what is it?' Mary walked through from the kitchen and handed him a plate of toast.

'Thanks, love, d'you know, I think he slept in the bus shelter all night, poor chap, I'm sure I saw him walking off towards the shop a few minutes ago,' Archie shook his head sadly, 'I should have done something.'

'Who? Who did? What's going on, love?'

Archie finished telling his wife about Jeff and they fell silent, thinking about his situation.

Linzi Carlisle

Mary stood up, filled with a sense of happy determination. 'Just because we're skipping Christmas this year doesn't mean that we can't help someone out.' Her mind was whizzing through a jumble of thoughts – they had some old clothes of Richard's in the garage (clothes deemed unsuitable by Sandy and thus destined for the charity shop, via Mary, whom Richard had somewhat sheepishly asked to do the deed on his behalf) – they had a spare room with a bed already made up (just in case it was needed) – they had food in the fridge freezer (not much, and nothing special, but she could always pick up a few bits at Joan's shop) – they were in a position to help someone in need and none of their own family appeared to want or need them.

There, she'd said it, well, in her head, not out loud, the thought that had been hovering in the back of her mind for days – their own kids didn't want or need them, certainly not over Christmas. It was partly the reason why she'd felt like ignoring Christmas this year, if they treated it as just another day, then there was less chance of feeling hurt and lonely about being forgotten about, less chance of disappointment when their own children declined their parents' invitations to lunch or tea, or even to pop in for a sherry for a little while, and less chance of feeling sad inside. And of course, the grandkids would never come of their own volition, that was down to Susan, and Susan had obviously got their Christmas all worked out, as had Richard, and Helen. She'd never share these thoughts with Archie though, wouldn't want to upset him, and maybe she'd got it all wrong, maybe the kids just led busy lives and struggled to fit in time to see their parents, even though they wanted to.

'Get your coat on, if we're going to catch him before he disappears, we need to move fast.'

'You're saying we should invite him to stay with us? But we don't know anything about him,' Archie tried to keep up with Mary and what she was saying to him as they walked towards the convenience store.

'You said he had a nice face, didn't seem like a criminal, or something like that, and you've always been good at reading people, so I trust you, besides, what on earth is the poor man going to do? It's Christmas Eve, Archie, he needs a bed to sleep in and some food in his belly. What's the worst that can happen? He can say no, or he can come into our home for a couple of nights.' Mary pushed the door open and walked into the convenience store, smiling at Joan.

'Hi, Mary, Archie, how are you both? All ready for Christmas?'

'We're actually skipping it this year,' Mary nodded, 'the kids are all busy with their own lives, and we're pleased for them, they've got friends and families, or new boyfriends, and our son's off on holiday with his wife, so we thought we'd enjoy a nice quiet time without all the usual headaches of jostling for turkeys and hams and preparing a whole load of complicated vegetable dishes to keep everyone happy, you know what it's like?'

'Actually, not really,' Joan's face was sad for a split second, 'I used to, of course, before Kev, well, before Kev died...'

Mary's face was sympathetic as she cursed inwardly for not thinking about the woman's situation, 'I'm sorry, I've put my foot in it.'

'Not at all,' Joan hurried to reassure, 'it's not something I go on about much, and Nigel and I are getting there, each year gets a little easier, this'll be the third...'

Archie wandered down the aisle, having spotted Jeff lurking at the back of the store, 'Jeff, hello again.'

Wiping his mouth as he finished the second sausage roll, Jeff looked up in surprise, 'Hello, Archie, isn't it? I must thank you again for the meal last night, it was really kind.'

'A pleasure, truly, now tell me, did you stay at your friend's last night in the end?'

No point in lying, he'd seen him from his window, he thought as he swigged the last of his tea, 'Turns out he moved away just a few days ago, must have been some mix up in communications,' he gave a rueful smile, 'so I'll be moving on and sorting something out today, it was a bit too late last night to do anything.'

'Now, you can say no if you want, I know you don't know us, but we're not complete old bores, and we've got an empty spare room and a comfy bed and no-one in need of it over Christmas,' putting his hands out to fend off Jeff's immediate instinct to refuse the offer, Archie played his trump card. 'My wife's the one to say no to, and believe me, she doesn't take no sitting down,' he grinned amiably. 'Come and meet her.'

Mary and Joan had been having a whispered conversation as Joan had filled her in on what little she'd observed about the man and, as if on cue, they both looked up.

'You must be Jeff,' Mary gave him a big smile, liking his face instantly, 'Archie's told me all about you, say you'll come and stay, just for a couple of nights if you want, it won't be a fancy Christmas, we're giving it a miss this year, but you'll be warm and fed.' She stopped to draw breath, looking at him hopefully.

'I don't know what to say, you don't know anything about me, I couldn't possibly impose...'

'We know all we need to know,' Archie chimed in, 'you're a chap having a bit of a struggle, your friend's let you down and it's Christmas Eve, and cold as anything, to boot.'

10

Skipping Christmas in Holly Crescent

'Did your husband tell you I've been in prison?' Jeff's eye looked directly into Mary's.

'He did, and right there, that's why we know everything is alright. If you had something terrible to hide, you'd never have told him. Say yes, Jeff, and Archie will take you home and settle you in while I pick up a few bits of shopping, we've even got some of my son's old clothes which will fit you.' And they would fit him, perfectly, she thought happily, having assessed his approximate size beneath his jacket.

'Well, yes then, if you're sure, I'd be very grateful,' he submitted, feeling relief wash over his body at the thought of a warm house and a bed for a night or two.

'That's settled then,' Mary clapped her hands happily, 'Archie, you two men go off home and I'll be back shortly. Jeff can have a hot bath while you get that suitcase of Richard's clothes out of the garage.'

Stopping to smile and thank Joan for the tea and sausage rolls, 'I'll pay you back, you did me a kindness, thanks,' Jeff followed his new friend from the store and together they walked the short distance to number nine.

'That's amazingly kind of you,' Joan stared at Mary after they'd left, 'inviting a stranger into your home. He seems very nice, I wonder what happened in his life?

'We might never know, it'll be up to him to tell us if he wants to, but no matter, no-one should be out alone in the cold at this time of year. Now, tell me what you and Nigel are doing for Christmas, we might not be doing anything but it's still fun to hear others' plans.'

Joan grinned, 'I'm just looking forward to the day off tomorrow. Not having to get up at six o'clock and spend the day in the shop will be bliss, having a nice cooked brekkie, lazing around and having something easy in the evening. He's a good lad, Nigel, never complains, although I do worry about him sometimes, he spends a lot of time on his own...'

Should she? Would she want to? They didn't really know each other apart from the odd casual chat in the shop, and maybe she'd just want to spend the time with her son, but what if she'd welcome some company... and it would be nice for Jeff to have someone else to talk to...

'This is probably going to sound really weird, like I'm some kind of crazy person...' Mary began.

'You can say no, I promise I won't be offended, not at all, but if you'd like some company then we'd love to have you both. It won't be Christmassy, we haven't got any decorations up, and there'll be no festive fare, but, well-' inspiration hit, 'you'd actually be helping us out, what with Jeff being with us.'

'But we'd be in your way, I wouldn't want us to be a bother.'

'Take a minute to think about it while I pick up a few bits, no pressure.' Mary picked up a basket and inspected the discounted items in the fridge. Some sausage rolls would be nice, although she could make some homemade ones, she thought, a small frisson of excitement bubbling up inside her.

'Do you have any frozen puff pastry?'

'We do, and the answer's yes, if you're sure.'

'I'm two hundred percent sure, 'Mary beamed, 'and two hundred percent happy that you've said yes. Now, I'll need pastry, tins of tomatoes, onions, some packs of sausages, oh, and some bacon for breakfast tomorrow. Perhaps I should get some more eggs...' She paused as a thought occurred to her, 'I'll need something for lunch and dinner today, too, now, I've got bread rolls in the freezer, but perhaps some cheese and ham, that'll sort lunch...' she tried to think what she could get out for dinner.

'There's a load of mini lasagnes for half price, I was going to use some for tomorrow, tip them into a dish and add more cheese, it sounds a bit sad, I know, but it would be something easy for you...'

'No, it's a great idea, thank you, I think I'll do that.'

The two women surveyed Mary's pile of shopping bags, 'You'll never get that home on your own.' As she spoke, the doorbell dinged, 'Oh, here's Nigel.' Joan smiled at her son, 'Did you pick up some good books, love?'

'I did, thanks for the money, Mum, you didn't have to do that. Tracy said I can take the puppy for a walk with her, is that okay?'

'Course it is, but could you do me a favour first? Could you just help Mary across the road with her shopping? We're going to join them tomorrow for a bit, with our new friend, Jeff. Mary, are you sure I can't bring anything?'

'Just yourselves, and why not come in the morning and have breakfast with us - if I'm cooking bacon and eggs for three it might as well be for five? Then you can help me cobble up a meal for us all for later with all these bits and pieces, plus I've got a huge chicken pie sitting in my fridge that I made and which wasn't needed last night. Oh, I'll need some more potatoes, I almost forgot.'

Joan shook her head, there's about three sad specimens left, I'm afraid. What if I bring some bags of frozen chips?'

Linzi Carlisle

'Why not?' Mary laughed, 'it'll be the weirdest Christmas dinner ever, well, not Christmas dinner, of course, but you know what I mean.'

As they walked to her house, Mary asked about the puppy, 'So who's Tracy? Does she live around here? Is it her new puppy?'

Nigel was enthusiastic, 'She lives in the flats, like us, but he's not hers, she's just fostering him over Christmas. He's really cute, Mum gave her a basket and a blanket for his bed, yesterday. Tracy works in the library, that's where I went this morning to buy some books in the sale.'

'Puppies and books, we're going to have lots to talk about tomorrow, Archie and I love dogs, we used to have a little Sheltie, Gemma her name was, such a gentle little soul, I still miss her. And books, well, you must ask Archie to show you all the books up in the attic, there must be about four boxes of them up there gathering dust. You'd be welcome to take any that you liked the look of.' Nigel's eyes lit up, much to Mary's pleasure.

'Does Tracy live on her own?'

Nigel nodded, 'She's in one of the one-bedrooms, I think she's quite shy.'

'I tell you what, why don't you and Tracy give our door a knock when you go for your walk, if it's not too far for the little pup, I'd love to see him.'

'Okay, sure.'

They dropped all the bags in the kitchen and Mary thanked Nigel, eliciting a promise from him that he'd show her the puppy.

'Where's Jeff? Did you settle him in? Did you give him the clothes to sort through?'

'All sorted, he's in the shower, the clothes are in the spare room, and before you ask, I put some of my underpants and socks in there, I realised the poor chap would probably be embarrassed to ask.'

'You, Archie Nugent, are a star,' Mary reached up and kissed him. 'As soon as he's down I'll pop an extra blanket on the bed for him, just in case he's cold. Then you must make some tea for you both and, oh, can you get a pack of rolls out of the freezer for me while I get this shopping put away? I'll need you two men out of my way, I've got lots to do in the kitchen.'

Archie took in the piles of shopping bags, before looking at his wife quizzically, 'That's a lot of food for three...'

'Actually, it's going to be five of us,' Mary had the grace to look sheepish, 'I know I should have asked you but she was going to be on her own with her son, and it really is very hard for them, what with her being a young widow...'

'Who are we talking about?'

'Joan, from the shop, and Nigel who was just here helping with the shopping bags, they're going to come for breakfast and stay for dinner. It'll be nice to have more company and not just us on our own with Jeff, don't you think? He doesn't want to be stuck on his own with us two, poor man.'

'Are you sure you're not trying to turn this into an actual Christmas?' Archie eyed his wife.

'Of course not, we're not doing Christmas, remember?'

'I remember. So, it's just a few people spending the day together for no particular reason?'

'Exactly,' nodding happily, Mary began putting the shopping away, a small smile in her eyes as she hummed softly.

Archie walked out of the kitchen, shaking his head. Was that a Christmas carol that his wife was humming?

'I need to use the bathroom!' Michaela banged on the door in frustration, 'Curtis, get out of there. Will somebody help me please?' Her voice became shrill as she looked around helplessly.

She was hating every minute of being here, it was all rubbish, she couldn't even have time on her own there was always someone else around. All her friends were posting cute photos on Instagram of their Christmas shopping, walking in the woods (yeah, like Rachel Hounslow ever went for a walk in the woods before, but she had a pink bobble hat with matching gloves and suddenly there she was, little woodland babe of the year), ice skating, sharing hot chocolate with boyfriends, it was driving her mad. And she was stuck here and she couldn't even get in the bathroom to take a selfie. She'd be forgotten about. Her heart thudded, in just a few days she'd have lost all her popularity, her followers would lose interest and drop her... 'OPEN THE DOOR NOW.'

'Michaela, keep it down, what's all the fuss about?' Her dad climbed the stairs, still wearing his dressing gown.

Skipping Christmas in Holly Crescent

'It's Curtis, he's been in the bathroom for half an hour and he's ignoring me.'

Patrick banged his fist on the door, 'Curtis, open the door. Now!'

The door opened slowly and Curtis peered around it at them, covered in white foam.

'What have you been doing? Is that my shaving foam? You little blighter, come here.'

'Let him be, he's just having a bit of fun,' Louise appeared, laughing at her son's appearance. 'Trying to look like Father Christmas, were you, love?' She turned to Michaela, 'Take a picture, he looks so cute, you can put it on your Instagram.'

'It'd ruin my whole theme, and anyway, I haven't got time, I need to use the bathroom.'

'Hold on, hold on, let's just get Curtis cleaned up first. Have I got any more shaving phone, Lou? No? Oh, great. You'll have to be quick, Micky, I need to get showered and dressed.'

'Did you tell them yet?' Louise's voice whispered urgently to Patrick as Michaela closed the bathroom door in relief. Tell them what, she wondered?

Susan woke up and turned to look at her boyfriend sprawled beside her and still out for the count. Somehow, she'd got through the evening, but it had been horrible. Why did Trevor have to work in public relations for fashion? The agency earned its money by promoting small, up and coming fashion brands for young Millennials, and every staff member, both male and female, was a walking advert for style, youth, and bony hips. Well, not Trev, he was one of the older ones, but he still looked good for thirty-six.

Slipping quietly out of bed, Susan crept into the bathroom and took her tee shirt off, turning to stand in front of the mirror. It wasn't completely dreadful, not for forty, she'd seen worse... although not last night. She pinched the excess flesh on her hip sadly, before turning to assess her behind, regretting it instantly as depression threatened to creep in.

They had to attend Trevor's boss's Christmas Eve party this afternoon, beginning with drinks and canapés at four o'clock, followed by something described as 'fashion show fun' on the invitation, whatever that was, and then, finally, dinner and dancing to round off the night. Yet again she needed something to wear and her wardrobe wasn't going to magically offer her up a perfect outfit. She'd have to go shopping for something. On Christmas Eve! What were the chances that she'd actually find something at this late stage? Zero, probably.

What she needed was a pair of Bridget Jones pants to hold everything in nicely and firmly, but then Trevor would see them when she got undressed, which was hardly sexy. Sighing, she turned on the shower taps and waited for the water to heat up. At least on Christmas Day she could wear something comfortable. Or could she? The thought alarmed her – she'd never met Trevor's parents before, this was the first time, so it was... important to make the right impression. Her shoulders sank.

Andrew and Dulcie Hope, at number ten Holly Crescent, were up with the larks, showered, dressed, breakfasted, and on their second cup of tea, when the phone rang. They looked at each other in surprise. It could be Gwyneth, calling to let them know they were about to get on the train, but no, they checked the time on their watches, they'd already be on their way. Frowning slightly, Andrew picked up the phone as Dulcie stood beside him.

'Oh, Gwyneth, hello, is everything-? Yes, yes, I see, well, don't you worry about us, and you're sure he's alright? Here's Dulcie, you take care now, sorry we won't be seeing you both, you have a nice Christmas now.'

Dulcie snatched the phone, 'Gwyn? What's happened? Are you alright? And Alasdair? Oh, he didn't, oh, no, he didn't, oh, he hasn't. Is he in pain? But nothing's broken? Are they sure? And he's coming home today? You poor things, no, don't you worry about us at all, we'll miss you both terribly, of course, but we'll be fine, you both take care now, and send our love to Alasdair. You just keep safe and have a nice, quiet Christmas.'

Disappointment showed all over her face as she turned to her husband, 'Poor Alasdair slipped on the wretched ice in their driveway as he was walking to the taxi. Went down with a terrible bang, Gwyneth said. It's left him badly shaken, he hit his head, so they took him to hospital, but they don't think he's broken anything, but he'll just be badly bruised and very sore. At least they're letting him go home soon, and he must rest, poor old thing. It's no fun being our age, is it? We have to be so careful. Oh, I do wish he'd watched his feet on the ice. Such a shame for them both, I hope their Christmas isn't too miserable, I mean, Gwyneth's not got any food in or anything, seeing as they were coming to us. But she's a sensible woman, I'm sure she's got plenty of things in the freezer, and it's just for a couple of days, it does tend to get rather blown out of proportion doesn't it, the whole Christmas thing? Just look at us, a couple of silly old fools with a Christmas tree all shiny and bright, a jolly Christmas cake in the larder, more food than we know what to do with and

13

no one to share it all with now. Well,' she picked up their now cold cups of tea, to take them into the kitchen, 'I hope you're feeling hungry, you're going to have to eat a lot of pigs in blankets.'

The sun was beginning to go down in Phuket and Richard took the beach towels from Sandy, rolling them up and shoving them into the basket. They hadn't talked the whole day, she, because she was in such a bad mood with him, and he, well, because he was being spineless. But now, as they waited to cross the busy street running alongside the beach, to return to their hotel, Sandy opened her mouth.

The vitriolic flow lasted the whole way back to their hotel as Sandy listed his failings regarding their holiday, hardly stopping to draw a breath. The words swarmed around him, barely registering in his weary brain, the odd phrase hitting its mark and stinging painfully.

'Absolute dump; building site; one star if that; cheapskate; you've totally let me down; terrible food; I wonder what I'm doing with you; worst Christmas ever; don't even take care of yourself; after everything I gave up for you...'

The entered their room, noses wrinkling slightly at the unmistakeable smell of damp, and Richard opened the balcony door fully to air the room.

'They haven't even made our bed, or changed the towels, they're still wet, and they haven't touched our tea mugs. No housekeeping, Richard. You've brought me to a place with no housekeeping even, I can't tell anyone about this, it's mortifying. What are you going to do about it? We can't stay here.' She stood with her hands on her hips, scowling at him, as her phone pinged and she tapped on the screen, reading something, a small smile hovering on her lips as her fingers flew over the small keyboard, her phone making tiny bleeping sounds at each touch.

Richard pulled the sheet straight on the bed, tucking it under the thin mattress, before pulling the duvet up and smoothing it with his hands. He placed the pillows on top and flung himself down on his side of the small, double bed. 'You're right, we can't stay here.' It felt like such a relief to say it, 'We'll leave tomorrow.'

But Sandy misunderstood, her face breaking into a happy grin, 'Oh, darling, I knew you'd agree with me. I'll start looking for a hotel straightaway. It should be five stars at least, a suite, I think, I wonder if any have their own private pools? And one of those places that has about three different restaurants, and a pool bar, and boutiques in reception selling gorgeous clothes and perfume and stuff. Oh, honey, I'm, so excited.' She threw herself down beside him, hugging him and reaching up to kiss him enthusiastically.

His pretty, young, money-grabbing, and possibly cheating on him, wife, had a skin like a rhinoceros. 'You go and shower first, I'll have a look on my phone, and then we'll go and have a drink before dinner, okay?'

He checked flights, disappointed to see that the only available flight left at midday the following day, Christmas Day, arriving at Heathrow at midday on Christmas Day, due to the time difference. His finger hovered over the button as he deliberated over whether to book it or not. He could use his emergency credit card which Sandy knew nothing about – thank goodness, otherwise that would be maxed out along with all his other cards.

How bad was it bail on your wife while on holiday? Really bad, a voice inside his head replied. Inexcusable.

Her phone was laying on the bed where she'd dropped it in her excitement, before she went to shower and he picked it up, checking the bathroom door. Had he reduced himself to the kind of man who spied on his wife? Slowly, he slid his finger across the screen and clicked on the last opened message, reading the last few messages in the thread, before closing it again and replacing her phone on the bed.

The shower was still running, which meant he'd have no hot water, but he didn't really care about that too much. He picked up his phone and booked himself the last available flight home for Christmas Day. Now he just had to get through tonight. Then he could give his not so darling wife the biggest Christmas surprise ever, he thought grimly.

Tracy Miller looked worriedly down at the little puppy, 'I think he's walked far enough, he needs carrying now.'

'I'll carry him,' Nigel bent down and picked up the wriggling pup, holding him close and burying his nose in his fur. 'Why do they always smell of coffee?'

'I don't know, it's weird that,' Tracy smiled, 'so who's your friend who wants to see the puppy?'

'Here it is, number nine, her name's Mary, and he's Archie, we're spending Christmas Day with them, but it's not actually Christmas Day because they're not doing Christmas this year, Mum said, so it's just a normal day. But Mum's looking forward to it, said it'll be nice to have some company, and they've got loads of books. What are you doing?'

Skipping Christmas in Holly Crescent

'Me? Oh, I'll just be at home, and I've got this little boy to keep me company, that's why I didn't mind fostering him over Christmas, gives me someone to talk to.'

Nigel rang the doorbell and they waited for the door to open.

Helen forced her eyes open, a pounding headache making her groan in despair. She reached for her water, leaning up on her elbow and gulping greedily from the bottle, before drooping back dramatically on the bed. She needed sustenance, could murder a fried breakfast, but of course, she couldn't actually have that. 'What time is it?'

'Twelve,' a loud yawn came from her flatmate Bianca's room, who appeared in person a few seconds later, tying her robe around her. 'I'm starving, have we got anything to eat?'

'I think there are some rice cakes in the cupboard,' stretching, Helen crawled from her bed, 'and please tell me we have coffee.'

Black coffee and dry rice cakes consumed, the two women collapsed in armchairs and discussed the previous night in detail before Helen announced, 'I think I'll go back to bed for a couple of hours, get some more beauty sleep,' she dragged herself up and went to sleep off her hangover. 'Wake me at six, babe.'

Michaela and Matthew Chavers sat together on the sofa, staring at their father, 'Nobody wants us around, Mum doesn't want us, you don't want us, Louise certainly doesn't want us,' Michaela's voice rose, 'what are we supposed to do then?' Secretly she felt thrilled, they were going back home which was loads better than being stuck here, at least she could meet up with her friends.

'That's not true, we all want you, but Louise's mum's had a turn and we have to go to her. Look, I'll make it up to you, I promise, but you need to get your bags ready. I'll call your mum and get her to come and collect you.'

She was overheating in the changing room, could feel herself sweating. Susan removed the red dress, thankful that she hadn't fastened every one of the small buttons running down the back. It probably wouldn't have fit anyway, if she'd done that. Time was running out, she should be at home getting ready and she needed to talk to Trevor, make sure that everything was alright between them, she was acutely aware that she'd been decidedly stroppy with him when they'd got home last night, or rather, this morning. Eyeing the black shift dress with the flowing sleeves, she removed it from the hanger and struggled into it, facing the mirror bleakly.

The sleeves hid a multitude of sins, she'd give them that, but her stomach rolls were accentuated by the fit of the dress. It was no good. But what was she going to do? She had time to rush to one more shop and then she'd have to give up. Her phone rang and she took it from her bag. What did Patrick want? She hadn't got time for this. Please don't let one of the kids be sick.

'What is it, Patrick?' she asked breathlessly as she tried to wriggle out of the dress.

'You sound out of breath, caught you at the gym, have I?'

Why did he always have to be so sarcastic? 'No, I'm just busy, it's Christmas Eve and I've got lots to do. What's the problem? Is it one of the kids?'

'Both of them, actually,' his voice was a little embarrassed, 'I know I said I'd have them for tonight and tomorrow night, but something's come up...'

'No way, you promised, besides, Trevor and I have important plans and I can't leave the kids on their own, Matthew's only thirteen for goodness sake.' Pulling on her leggings with one hand, she looked around for her jumper, wishing she'd worn something thinner, she was about to spontaneously combust.

'Lou's mum's had a turn and we have to go to her, I'm sorry, Suze, but it's out of my hands. They prefer being with you anyway. Can you come and get them? We have to leave in an hour, it's a long drive.'

'No, I can't!' her voice had risen by about twenty decibels. 'I can't cope with this, Patrick, I cannot believe you're doing this to me.' Thinking rapidly, she made a decision, 'I'll send a taxi for them, they can go to my mum and dad. They won't mind, they're probably not doing anything much.' The thought made her pause guiltily, she hadn't even considered what her parents were doing for Christmas and whether they were on their own or not. Perhaps they were going to Richard's, she thought with relief, well, the kids could just go along too.

Ending the call, she tapped out a message to her mum, knowing that she should have called, but it would take too long, her mum would have a million questions and worries and she just didn't have the time to deal with her right now. Next, she ordered a taxi to collect the children and take them to Holly Crescent, before hurriedly gathering up her bits and exiting the changing room in a hot fluster.

15

Linzi Carlisle

Mary handed the puppy back to Nigel with a longing smile, 'Oh, he makes me miss our little Gemma even more. So, Tracy, you live at the flats? I think I've seen you walking past a few times, and you work at the library, Nigel was telling me?'

Tracy nodded shyly, 'Yes, that's about it, not much more to tell,' she looked up and gave Mary a quick smile.

'Well, I think it sounds fascinating, so would Archie, we both love books, although as I told Nigel, we've got boxes of them up in the attic with no shelves to put them on, some of them are quite old. Our house before was a bit bigger, but once the children grew up and left home, we found we were rattling around in it a bit too much, so we moved here. It's nice and snug at least.' She noticed Tracy's eyes light up with interest at the mention of the books, and made a snap decision.

'What are you and this little pup doing tomorrow? Now don't tell me you're spending the day in your flat alone?'

Shrugging, Tracy nodded, 'I don't really know anyone around here yet, I only moved in a few months ago. But it's okay, I don't mind, I mean, it's just another day...'

Mary beamed, 'Exactly, just another day. Which is why you should both come and join our motley crew tomorrow. How about it? We're not having Christmas, we're skipping it altogether, but that doesn't mean we can't be neighbourly and enjoy a little company.' She could see Tracy wavering. 'It would be such a treat to have a little puppy here to entertain us, what do you say?'

'D'you mean it? I mean, are you sure?'

Nigel was nodding like mad, 'Say yes, I'll get to spend the day with the puppy and loads of books, it'll be much better than a normal Christmas Day.'

'Alright then, it would be really nice, thank you. I'll have to bring his bed and food with me, is that okay? Only he gets tired and hungry just about every hour.'

'I'll come and help you carry everything, you can come with me and Mum in time for breakfast.'

'That's right, eggs and bacon and loads of toast and tea, the best way to start the day,' humming happily, Mary waved them off and closed the door, walking slowly back into the lounge where Archie and Jeff were sitting deep in conversation. She hurried through to the kitchen as her oven timer pinged, and opened the door to remove her first batch of sausage rolls, expertly popping them onto a cooling rack. Slipping the next lot into the oven, she closed the door, set the timer, and considered the situation. She now had six people and a puppy joining them tomorrow, she thought with a happy flutter. Giving Christmas a miss was turning out to be quite interesting. But did she have enough food? Grabbing her coat, she informed Archie that she had to pop back to the shop for something she'd forgotten, and hurried along to the convenience store.

'Hello again,' Joan looked up in surprise as she served the last of her line of customers. It never ceased to amaze her how many people suddenly needed stuff at the last minute.

'Hi, Joan, I need some suggestions. It turns out that there'll be six of us tomorrow, the young girl, Tracy, and the little puppy, are going to spend the day with us all as well, isn't that wonderful?'

'Wow, yes, are you sure? Nigel and I don't need to–'

'Oh yes you do,' Mary grinned, 'you should have seen your son's face when Tracy agreed to come with the puppy. The only thing is, I think we might need some more food, I don't want anyone going hungry...'

Joan looked around doubtfully, 'It's been quite busy, there's not much left... um, how about pizza? Or is that just too weird? I've still got a box of them in the freezer out the back, although it's not very festive...'

'That's okay, we're not being festive, remember? Pizza will be great, how many should I get do you think? Maybe four if they're a decent size? And I'd better get some more bread, that's if there's any left,' she looked at Joan hopefully.

But Joan shook her head, 'The bread's all gone, I'm sorry, but I think there are some muffins, would they do? And there are still some garlic breads in the freezer.'

'Muffins, yes, I think so, yes, we can do something with those, and garlic breads are a great idea.' She looked down in surprise as her phone pinged, taking it out of her pocket to read the message from Susan. 'We'd better make it eight pizzas, it seems that my grandchildren are being sent to stay with us and are arriving within the hour, so they might want pizza tonight instead of my cheat's lasagne. It's all getting quite exciting, much more fun than stressing over Christmas Day lunch and dinner and all the decorations and stuff.'

Joan shook her head, laughing, 'It's starting to sound pretty hectic, and a lot like a normal Christmas to me.'

'Oh, it's nothing like a normal Christmas,' Mary shook her head, laughing, 'usually I'd have been stressing for days, worrying about buying the turkey, buying fresh vegetables as close to the day as possible and

16

Skipping Christmas in Holly Crescent

struggling with complicated recipes for something to impress everyone with, washing all my best china ready for the big meal, ironing my big tablecloth and hunting for nice serviettes and things, oh no, instead of all that we're just going to throw a whole lot of food on the table and enjoy each other's company, no stress, and no worrying, it's wonderful.'

Walking back, her arms loaded with the pizzas, the bag containing the muffins and garlic breads swinging from her arm, she pondered Susan's message. Her daughter's message had seemed harassed, as if she was under strain, and had clearly been tapped out in record time, judging by the typos. It would have been nice to have been *asked* if they'd mind having the children, but a sixth sense told her that her daughter was struggling and she wondered if she should give her a call to check that she was alright. And the poor children, sent from pillar to post for the festive holidays, and now they'd be stuck spending two completely Christmas free nights with their grandparents.

And where were they going to sleep? She stopped abruptly in the middle of the pavement. They had one spare room, which was currently occupied by Jeff, and they certainly couldn't boot him out, absolutely not, he'd only just settled in, and the poor man was in need. As were her grandchildren though...

There was the tiny boxroom, but it didn't have one bed, let alone two. Perhaps if they moved out the boxes containing her sewing material, her sewing machine table which was tucked against the wall between the small desk that Archie sometimes used – which would have to come out too – and the chest of drawers. There was just about space on the landing for the furniture, and the boxes could go in the attic. That would work, she nodded to herself, muttering, unaware of the strange looks Archie was giving her from the window. And then, she thought triumphantly, they could use the foam sleeping mats and sleeping bags which had ended up in their garage after Sandy had informed Richard that if he thought she'd ever go camping then he needed his brain testing. There was his old tent in the garage as well, she laughed to herself, which might come in handy if they needed to accommodate any more people overnight. Pleased that she'd washed the sleeping mats and sleeping bags before packing them up neatly in dustbin bags, she turned to walk through their gate.

'Mary, what on earth's going on, have you lost your marbles?' Archie stood in the open doorway staring at his wife, 'Why are you carrying a pile of pizzas? Here, give them to me and come inside, it's freezing out here.'

'We need to hurry, we've got so much to do, there's absolutely no time to waste,' Mary marched through to the kitchen, checking on her sausage rolls, before opening the freezer door and turning to her husband, 'Pass me those pizzas will you, love?'

'I think Mary's gone mad,' Dulcie Hope turned away from their front window, 'I've just seen her standing in the middle of the pavement, talking and laughing to herself, and holding a whole load of what looked like pizzas. What on earth is she doing? And I'm sure I saw a strange man go in there earlier, with Archie, and he never left. But pizzas? And so many. They've put up no decorations and now it looks like they're going to live on pizza for days. Are they not even aware that it's Christmas Day tomorrow? It's all extremely out of character for Mary.'

With Archie and Jeff following her instructions, Mary called her daughter. The phone rang until it went to voicemail so she tried again, feeling concerned.

'Mum, I really haven't got time to talk, did you get my message?' Susan twisted her neck to see her behind in the mirror.

'Yes, dear, but it's all a bit last minute, are you sure everything's alright, you sound rather strained? I'm worried about you, love.'

'Of course I'm strained, Mum, it's Christmas Eve, I mean, who isn't?' she hissed into the phone. Her bottom didn't look too enormous, the extra support on the trousers was quite amazing. Now she just needed to decide on a top. The door of the changing room flew open and the sympathetic face of the sales assistant appeared around it.

'How are the trousers? Oh, they look fabulous, very slimming. I've brought you two more tops to try on, but you'll need to be quite quick if you don't mind, we've got a queue of people waiting, it being Christmas Eve and everything...'

'Yes, thank you, I will,' beginning to feel too hot again, Susan realised that her mother was still on the phone. 'Mum, sorry I have to go. I'll collect the kids on Boxing Day, okay?'

'You're not out shopping for clothes at this time in the afternoon? What are your plans for Christmas, darling, you never actually told us? You sound terribly flustered, why don't you find somewhere to sit down and have a cup of tea?'

'Mum, I have to go,' she spoke through her gritted teeth, 'I'll tell you all about our Christmas when I get the kids, how's that? Okay, bye, Mum.' Relieved to have got her mother off the phone, she turned her attention to the tops hanging in front of her, ignoring the little voice in her head reminding her that she hadn't even wished her parents a Happy Christmas, or even asked how they were or whether they'd had any plans.

'Alright, dear, enjoy yourselves, and you know, we'd love to meet your new man, Trevor, isn't it?' Mary checked her phone screen and realised that Susan had gone. All that stress, it wasn't doing her any good, if only her daughter had given her mum a minute to chat, she could have told her that they were skipping Christmas entirely and felt so much the better for it.

Right, now how had the men got on with all the furniture moving? Bustling up the stairs, Mary ran through the ingredients for her famous piped biscuits; she had plenty of margarine, and the plain flour and cornflour were in the cupboard, icing sugar – yes, she checked the items off on her fingers – vanilla essence and some glacé cherries – that was it. She'd make a double batch once she'd given the box room a quick hoover, with a bit of luck she'd get them in the oven before the children arrived. And then she'd get the beds made up for the kids...

'Mary, are you listening to me?' Archie wiped his brow, the chest of drawers had been heavier than he'd thought. 'Don't you think you need to have a sit down and a cup of tea? In fact, I insist, you've been on the go for hours. You go and put the kettle on and I'll be down to make some tea after we've got these boxes out of the way, I expect Jeff could do with a cuppa, couldn't you, Jeff?' He looked up at the open attic hatch as Jeff's smiling face appeared.

'A cuppa sounds great, thanks, I'll just stack the rest of these boxes. Tell you what, you go down as well, Archie, I can manage on my own and you probably need a break.'

'Well, that's true, we're neither of us as young as we were, thanks Jeff, see you downstairs in a bit then.'

Jeff rested on his haunches for a moment, smiling to himself and shaking his head. He could never have imagined that instead of staying with his old mate, Russell, who wasn't so much of a mate, seeing as he'd upped and gone and left him with nowhere to go, he'd be in the spare room of a very sweet, older couple, helping them prepare for a Christmas that they insisted on telling him they were skipping this year. He raised his eyebrows – if that was skipping Christmas then he dreaded to imagine how chaotic it was when they actually went full throttle with the turkey and the tree and everything. He took a final glance around, satisfied that he'd stacked everything neatly, his eyes falling on a box labelled Christmas decorations. Kind of a shame not to put a few up, he thought, but clearly they wanted none of the festive stuff this year. Climbing down the ladder, he closed the hatch. Mary and Archie's grandchildren would be arriving soon and the thought made him think of his own son, Luke. He wondered what he was doing for Christmas. Probably being spoiled by his ex-wife's new boyfriend, he thought bitterly. Spotting the hoover on the landing, he switched it on and quickly hoovered the box room, before going downstairs for a welcome cup of tea.

'Where've you been? I was about to call you. I woke up to find you missing but my head was killing me so I crawled into the shower. Hasn't helped much,' Trevor's face was sheepish.

'No, well, it wouldn't, not after the amount you had last night,' she was being prissy, she knew, but couldn't seem to help it. 'Enjoyed yourself did you, last night?' Why could she not keep her mouth shut?

'Don't start, Suze, not now, we had a good night, didn't we?' Trevor rubbed his wet hair gingerly, wincing.

'I don't know, did we? Perhaps we should ask Pam, she might know.'

'What's that supposed to mean? You know what? Forget it, we have to leave in about half an hour. Are you ready?'

Susan's eyes were wild, 'Do I look ready? Look at me, I'm a mess, I need to shower and get dressed, do my hair and makeup...' her voice trailed off as she registered what Trevor had said about them leaving. 'Half an hour? That can't be right,' she looked at her watch, 'it's only two o'clock.'

'It's three o'clock, your watch must have stopped. This is important to me, Suze, it's my boss, you'd better hurry.'

Aghast, Susan began pulling her clothes off in a panic before rushing into the shower and hurriedly soaping her body. There was no time to wash her hair so she stuck her head under the water before stepping out and briskly drying herself. Leaving her hair for a moment, she tipped her new outfit onto the bed, groaning when she saw the crumpled top.

18

Skipping Christmas in Holly Crescent

'Cab's coming in ten minutes,' Trevor helpfully called from downstairs.

This couldn't be happening to her, not another disastrous party where she looked like something the cat had dragged in. She switched the iron on in the spare room, ran back to the bedroom and blasted the hairdryer, trying in vain to smooth her hair into obedience with her hand. The cab hooted outside as she finished ironing her top and she pulled it on as she hunted for hairspray. Throwing makeup into her handbag she rushed downstairs and out of the door, where Trevor waited impatiently.

'You look nice,' Trevor smiled at her once they were on their way, 'not bad for half an hour, imagine those girls at work, I bet they have to spend a couple of hours getting ready. They're high maintenance, that's what it's called, whereas I am a lucky man indeed, having a low maintenance girlfriend.'

Yeah, and they look a lot better for it, she thought silently, holding her mirror in one hand as she applied foundation with the other. 'Thank you,' he was trying to be nice and she didn't want them to fight, even though she had bridled slightly at being called low maintenance – was that some kind of backhanded compliment? 'So do you.' He did look nice, she thought, reaching across to squeeze his hand. A slight smell of perspiration reached her nose and, in horror, she realised that she'd forgotten to put deodorant on. And perfume.

The doorbell rang and Archie opened the door to their grandchildren, who stood on the doorstep, holding their bags and looking miserable. 'Come in, come in, here, give me one of those bags.'

'Where are all the Christmas decorations?' Michaela walked into the lounge, staring around at the room. Who are you?'

'This is Jeff, he's a friend of ours and he's staying with us for a couple of nights,' Mary beamed as she opened her arms and hugged her, before doing the same with Matthew.

'Doesn't your grandad get a hug?' Archie grinned, giving them both hugs. 'Say hello to Jeff.'

Jeff stood, smiling and feeling a little awkward, 'Hi, Michaela and Matthew, it's nice to meet you both.'

They murmured hellos and Michaela turned to go upstairs, 'Matt, bring the rest of our stuff up to our room, and you'd better have a shower if I have to sleep in the same bed as you.' Her Christmas was just getting worse and worse, she thought miserably.

'Er, you're in the boxroom,' Mary rushed to the stairs as Michaela disappeared from view.

Archie's face was slightly grim, 'I'll deal with this,' he put out a hand to still his wife. 'These kids could do with learning some manners.' He walked up the stairs to find Michaela staring into the spare room.

'Whose stuff is this?'

'We told you, Jeff's staying with us. Now, here's what's going to happen, you're going to put a smile on that pretty face of yours, and then you and Matthew and going to come out to the garage with me and Jeff, and find the bags with your Uncle Richard's old camping bits in. Then you're going to make up your beds in the boxroom. Uh uh,' Archie wagged his finger as she opened her mouth, 'no complaining, and no upsetting your grandma, she's happy to have you both here, we both are, but we've been busy preparing for your arrival and we're a little tired now.'

Mary hummed as she slid the tray of piped biscuits into the oven, it would be a really nice evening tonight, she thought happily, the kids would love having pizza, and the adults would enjoy the lasagne, or maybe they'd all just grab bits of each. And she'd pop a few sausage rolls out once the kids had got their beds sorted out, they'd like those with a cup of tea.

Archie looked around nonplussed as Jeff reached for another black bag, 'Maybe this one? No, hold on, that says blankets.' Jeff reached for a box, 'Are we sure they're in bags and not boxes?'

'That one says Christmas tree,' Matthew pointed out helpfully, 'so we should get it down, shouldn't we? Don't we need to put up the tree and all the decorations?'

'Well, the thing is, son, we're not having a Christmas this year, none of that fuss and bother, there was no real need as the whole family was busy doing other things and your grandma and I decided that we'd have a nice quiet time of it. Much less work all round,' Archie nodded knowingly.

'Found it,' Jeff threw a large black bag down to Matthew, who caught it, laughing. 'Look out, here's another, nearly got you.' He climbed down from the stepladder, grinning as Matthew struggled to hold the two big bags. 'Here, give me one of those, let's go and get you guys set up in your room.'

Matthew's face was screwed up in thought, 'But we're here and we're family, so don't we count, Grandad?'

Archie tousled his hair, 'Of course you do, love, I meant the grown-ups, I suppose.'

'Then why can't we have decorations up? I don't get it, I mean, me and Micky can do it if you and Grandma are too tired.'

'Count me out, it's all childish anyway, and I bet Grandma and Grandad's decorations are about a hundred years old. And stop calling me Micky or I'll start calling you Matty Fatty.'

'That's not the same thing, Micky's a nice name, why d'you have to be mean?'

Noticing the hurt that fleetingly creased Matthew's face, Jeff tried to distract them, 'Hello, what's this up on the rafters? Looks like an old bagatelle board.'

'Coo, that takes me back, tell you what, let's bring that in, might be a bit of fun later.'

Andrew Hope, acting on instructions from his wife, walked down the shared driveway as the group emerged from the garage, their arms filled with dustbin bags and a large wooden board. 'Afternoon, Archie, all set for Christmas?'

'Afternoon, Andrew, no Christmas for us, we're giving it a miss this year, decided we'd escape all the fuss and bother.'

Andrew's eyebrows ascended towards his shock of white hair, 'If you say so, although you look to be pretty busy from where I'm standing.'

Archie laughed, 'Well, we've got the grandkids, you know Michaela and Matthew, it was all a bit last minute, poor things, their mother's having a busy time of it and their father had some sort of family emergency, so here we are. Oh, and this is our friend Jeff, he's spending a couple of nights with us.'

'Looks like you've got quite the full house,' Andrew shook Jeff's hand, as Jeff wrestled with the bagatelle board under his arm.

'Are you and Dulcie having visitors for Christmas? Your tree looks nice in the window, by the way.'

'No, turns out we're just on our own, Dulcie's brother, Alasdair, had a fall this morning, just as they were leaving for the station. Not to worry, won't be the first time we've spent Christmas on our own, you get used to it when you don't have kids. Kind of feel a bit silly with the tree all decked out and on display, but it cheers us up, I suppose. Dulcie's upset, poor thing, trying not to show it, of course.'

'Sorry to hear that, well, we'd better get these kids set up with their beds, and you should go in, Andrew, it's icy out here, feels a bit like snow weather if you ask me. Give our love to Dulcie, won't you?'

'Snow? Brilliant.' Matthew's face lit up in excitement as Michaela grinned, thinking about possible photos she could take. If only she had a pretty bobble hat...

Susan kept her arms down by her side as much as possible as they greeted fellow guests of Trevor's boss, wondering how long she could leave it before finding her way to a bathroom. With a bit of luck she'd find some deodorant that she could borrow, maybe even some perfume.

'Trevor my man,' Dickson was clearly well oiled already as he approached them, his arms wide as he pulled the older man by almost twenty years into a hug. 'And the sultry Susan, welcome,' he enveloped Susan in an embrace, pulling her close so that her breasts were pressed against his chest.'

Awkwardly, she disentangled herself with a stiff smile, 'Hello, Dickson, thank you for having us.' Could she not relax a little? She sounded like a school mistress.

'And this is Ronnie, my girlfriend.' A thin, flat-chested blonde appeared by his side, smiling and giving limp handshakes to them both before wandering off, her stiletto heels digging into the thick pile carpet and leaving small holes with each step. 'Isn't she wonderful? Although a bit lacking in some departments, know what I mean, eh, Trev?' Dickson's eyes glanced at Susan's breasts as he winked, nudging Trevor, 'you're a lucky man.' Ronnie turned, looking back and raking her eyes scornfully down the length of Susan's body.

Her face flushed in embarrassment as Trevor laughed along loudly with his boss. Really, how could Trevor abide these people? And how about defending her honour? As his boss wandered off, she hissed in Trevor's ear, 'I need to use the bathroom, where is it?'

After a frantic hunt through the cupboard beneath the basin, hoping for something that she could spray under her arms, she admitted defeat. Stripping off her top and tucking the hand towel into her waistband, she leaned over the basin and washed under her arms, before patting them dry. Her eyes fell on the air freshener placed on top of the cistern. She couldn't, could she? Giving it a small squirt, Susan sniffed the air. It didn't smell too bad, sort of forest-like and a bit like a wet garden after the rain. Oh well, it was better than nothing. Lifting each arm she sprayed a generous amount into her armpits, flapping her arms to get it to dry, wincing as her skin stung slightly.

With her lipstick touched up, she fluffed her hair and resolutely left the bathroom, wondering how many hours it would be before they could acceptably leave.

She spied Trevor through the crowd at the bar and pushed her way through as his words reached her ears.

'You're looking gorgeous tonight, Pam, can I get you another drink?'

Pam's giggle floated through the air as she leaned in to Trevor, placing her hand on his arm, 'I'll have a Prosecco, darling.'

'Oh, hi, Suze, you know Pam? Pam, this is my girlfriend, Susan.'

'Susan, how are you? Enjoying the party?' Pam's eyes were already looking away from Susan as they scanned the room.

'So, Pam, I thought we might find a few minutes to talk about the new project...' Trevor handed her the glass of Prosecco.

'It's a party, Trevor, no boring work talk today, sweetie. Oh look, there's Laurence. Laurence, you handsome beast, Dickson was so impressed with your ideas for the new client...'

Trevor's face was despondent as Pam walked off, his eyes watching the young man wrap his arm around her waist and laugh knowingly at something she murmured in his ear.

'I'll have a Prosecco as well, please,' Susan spoke tightly to Trevor, her stomach knotted. How could he show his attraction to that woman so blatantly, while she, his girlfriend, was standing right here? Miserably she took the glass from him, gulping it down in one go.

'Steady on, Suze, have you eaten anything today?' Trevor's eyes were already roaming the room and he touched her arm, 'Give me a minute, okay?' He disappeared off through the growing throng and Susan turned back to the bar, she may as well have another drink.

The party wasn't so bad after all, she decided, a while later, as the small group gathered around her laughed at something witty she'd said. It had been witty, hadn't it? Her hand reached up to scratch furiously under her arm to ease the itching, burning sensation which was becoming increasingly sore. She should probably eat something though, she thought, reaching out a hand to grab a blini from the passing waiter but missing him as he continued, seemingly unaware of her existence. Well maybe she wouldn't eat anything then, she'd go the whole day with no food and lose a few pounds dramatically overnight. Then Trevor would fancy her again. She turned to share her decision with her new friends, but they'd dispersed into the surrounding crowd.

A tinkling glass sounded as the music was turned down low and Dickson hopped up onto a small podium. 'Thanks for coming, everyone, are you enjoying the party?'

Whooping cries of yes were joined by cheers and hand clapping and Susan shrieked delightedly.

'Loving it!'

A few eyes turned to glance in her direction and she forced herself to stop scratching her upper arm. The itching sensation was spreading.

'And here's the beautiful Ronnie who, together with the fabulous Pam, has organised tonight's fashion show fun. Let's give the girls a huge round of applause.'

Susan clapped enthusiastically, throwing in a whoop or two for good measure.

'So,' Dickson continued, 'Who's going to volunteer to walk the runway?'

'Me! Me!'

'We've got our first volunteer, come on up. And who else is going to join her?'

The crowd parted as Susan made her way towards the podium, wobbling slightly, but cheered on by some of the more raucous men in the gathering.

She was joined by a few of the other women, all feigning reluctance as they swished their hair and smiled perfectly at the photographer, who bounced around snapping enthusiastically.

'Let's not be sexist here, how about some of the guys? Okay, okay, I'll do it,' Dickson grinned as his name was chanted.

A couple of other men joined them, posing for the camera, and the music was turned back up as the group were directed through a curtain.

Everything was beginning to sound a little fuzzy, as if everyone was speaking to her from a distance, and Susan shook her head to clear it. 'Choose your outfit and get changed, ladies and gentlemen, we have two minutes until you're on. The loudest cheers will decide our fashion show model, and remember, it's all for fun, so enjoy yourselves.'

Blinking her eyes to focus her vision, which seemed a little off, she was surprised to see the others taking off their clothes with no embarrassment. They were rapidly dressing themselves in some of the outlandish garb that hung on the rail.

'One minute everyone.' Pam clapped her hands to speed everyone up.

'How about this?' Ronnie was beside her, holding out a sequined dress, 'it might fit.'

With nowhere to sit down, Susan managed a balancing act as she removed her boots and trousers, before tugging her top off over her head.

'Let's go people.' Pam was sending the others out through the curtain as the music boomed dramatically.

Linzi Carlisle

She pulled the dress down over her head, forcing her arms through the armholes and wriggled desperately as she tried to force it over her hips. Her knickers were sliding down and she hitched them back up while trying to get her boots back on. With a final scratch at her arms, she stumbled through the curtain, with a helpful shove from Ronnie.

'I love your sausage rolls, Grandma, they're the best,' Matthew shoved another one in his mouth appreciatively.

'Thank you, love. Jeff, another sausage roll?'

'Phew, I've had three, I'd better refuse, delicious though they are, I won't have any room for dinner.'

'Talking of which, it should all be just about ready. Now where is Michaela?'

'There's an Agatha Christie on the TV tonight, might be nice to watch it? Can't beat the old murder mysteries written years ago, so much better than half of the new stuff.' Archie folded the Radio Times, placing it back on the coffee table as he popped another sausage roll in his mouth.

'This is still a bit like Christmas if you think about it,' Matthew sprayed a few pastry crumbs in his enthusiasm, 'sausage rolls and old films on the tele.'

'I think it's a new version,' Archie picked up the magazine again, 'here we are, Murder on the Orient Express, yep, with that Branagh fellow and someone called Johnny Depp?'

'Johnny Depp? Can we watch it?' Michaela appeared in the lounge, leaning over the coffee table to grab a sausage roll. 'He's gorgeous.'

'I'm happy if everyone else is? Jeff, would you mind if we watched it?'

'Not at all, it's your house, please don't worry about me, I'm just grateful to be here. Extremely grateful, I can't thank you enough.' He smiled at Mary.

'Oh good, that settles it then. Right, dinner should be ready, Michaela would you like to give me a hand?'

'Alright.' Michaela followed her grandmother to the kitchen, her eyes glued to her phone.

'Why don't you put that down for a while, love? Is it your photo project? Have you put anything nice on there? Grandad would love to see it, did you know he used to enjoy photography as a hobby when he was young.'

'It's not the same thing, it's much more complicated.'

'Yes, well, I expect we're too old to understand it all. Here, take this pizza through, will you?'

Michaela finally looked up from her phone, 'Pizza? I don't think I've ever seen you serve up pizza for dinner in my life, Gran.'

Grinning, Mary lifted the dish of lasagne from the oven, 'We're having an Italian night, lasagne and pizza, courtesy of Joan, the lovely young lady from the convenience store, who gave me the idea. She's got a lovely son, Nigel, you'll meet him tomorrow, he must be about your age. He's a nice boy, very into his books, you'll have plenty to talk about, won't that be nice?'

'Boring,' Michaela carried the pizza from the kitchen, 'we'll have absolutely nothing to talk about.'

Cries of enthusiasm came from the dinner table as Matthew spotted the pizza, and Mary hummed happily as she removed the other pizza from the oven, popping everything on the table and fetching the basket of garlic bread to place in the centre with a final flourish, as hands reached hungrily to grab a slice of the hot, buttery, bread, amidst much laughter.

Opening her eyes, Helen was aware of the silence in the flat, and reached for her watch. Seven o'clock. Oh great, Bianca must still be asleep and now they'd have to get ready in record quick time. She looked up in surprise at the sound of the door opening, 'Bianca, is that you, darling? You didn't wake me.' She pouted as her flatmate walked in holding out a coffee.

'Peace offering, I popped out earlier and didn't want to wake you too early, then I got carried away looking at gorgeous floaty dresses and things, and the next thing I knew it was seven o'clock and I almost collapsed in horror. So here's some coffee to wake you up, with a tiny dash of cream, not much, I promise.' Placing the coffee down beside Helen's bed, Bianca turned and left the room, calling out, 'And now we must get ready, for tonight we party, baby.'

Smiling, Helen pushed herself up against her pillows and reached for her coffee, taking a delicious sip as she wondered when she'd last tasted cream. It wouldn't be so bad if she actually got acting roles, but to spend her whole time 'stage ready' and thin, so very thin, and to not even get work, well that was a little on the depressing side.

To make things worse, she had to constantly be seen at the right places, which was something her parents had never understood, and it cost a fortune, buying meals that she couldn't eat for fear of putting on weight, just so that she could sit in the restaurant of the moment, wearing the latest styles, keeping her hair styled

22

and makeup perfect at all times, and never forgetting to smile, not for a moment, because you can bet that would be the moment some sneaky photographer would take her picture.

Oh, who was she kidding? No photographer had even tried to take her photo, not for a couple of years, not since she'd appeared in the Christmas pantomime for the local hospital, which, coincidentally, corresponded with the last time she'd had actual acting work. Which hadn't been paid as it had been for charity. She grimaced at the thought of her overburdened credit cards, hoping that she had just enough credit on the one to pay for the enormously extravagant lunch tomorrow.

Alex had booked the lunch at Salvatore's and hadn't even asked her if she wanted to go or not, it was just assumed that their group would do his bidding. Of course, Alex was loaded - family money - so no problem for him, Zara had just finished a six month stint in a stage production of something called We Live in Boxes, which had apparently entailed lots of actual crouching in boxes on stage and occasionally popping up to list all the wrongs in the world, in German, for some bizarre reason, whilst wearing animal costumes – Zara had been a rabbit - the whole thing being the brainchild of some new kid on the block who seemed to be hugely popular with the critics. Zara had spoken of it scornfully, but it had paid nicely and as a result, she was exempt from their usual money worries right now. Helen had been jealous of her, actually jealous, had desperately wished that it was she who'd been chosen to squash herself into a box on stage for hours – the play was four hours long – dressed as a rabbit or a cat. And Bianca? Well, she was as poor as Helen, they both took casual work at theatres, working backstage, painting scenery, stitching up the oft ripped seams of costumes, sweeping up, making coffee, whatever was needed, anything to keep them close to the action, close to the temple of actordom, and when that failed there was always waitressing.

Which made it strange, then, that she'd just bought Helen a coffee with cream – a purchase they considered unnecessary unless under the most deserving of circumstances - such as a celebration when one or the other of them landed a role, no matter how small... But Bianca hadn't said a word if that was the case, in fact, she'd practically avoided Helen's eyes. She wandered through to Bianca's room, 'Which shop did you see the floaty dresses in?'

'What?' Bianca hurriedly rubbed body lotion into her legs, 'Oh, one of those boutiques, I can't remember the name right now, it'll come to me, I expect,' she gave a little laugh. 'You'd better hurry up and shower, we don't want to miss all the fun.'

Helen stood under the weak flow of water from the shower, pondering her flatmate. She was definitely hiding something, Bianca could act but one thing had always let her down and that was that she'd never been any good at laughing convincingly on stage, the sound having been compared once, quite cruelly by a critic, to the braying of a donkey. And Bianca had just softly brayed like a donkey, ergo Bianca had been acting, ergo Bianca was hiding something. But what? The water ran cold and she cursed, hurriedly rinsing the conditioner out of her hair as she began to shiver.

An hour later they left the flat, looking suitably fabulous, and climbed into their taxi for the short drive to Alex's rather sumptuous London residence, where the music could be heard pounding as they walked through the imposing gates and along the path to the front door, guided by twinkling Christmas lights.

'Darlings,' Alex swanned over as they entered, a glass of champagne in each hand, leaning in for air kisses as he studied their appearance, 'perfect, positively star like, the pair of you, here have some champers.' He handed them the glasses, 'What d'you think? I hired professional Christmas decorators, isn't it marvellous? Everyone who's anyone is here, so you must mingle. Mingle, girls.' Turning to go, he leaned into Bianca, 'Fabulous news, darling, Harry told me.'

'Oh look, there's Zara,' Bianca grabbed Helen's arm, steering her towards a group gathered beside an enormous Christmas tree.

Had she heard Alex correctly? Fabulous news? It was difficult to hear anything above the music, maybe she'd got it wrong. Pulled into the festive whirl, she forgot about it as they drank and danced and pretended to eat the nibbles.

The evening steadily descended into raucous chaos as the hours passed and Helen forced her way to the bathroom, opening the door and walking into the silence - the music being muted by the thickness of the wooden door – where she paused to admire the décor - it was like being in a hotel.

From her cubicle, she heard the door open and the pounding of the music, before it fell quiet again, apart from the voices of the two women chatting excitedly.

'Marvellous party, Alex really knows how to pull out all the stops.'

'Did you hear about Serena's pop-up theatre? It's going to be an absolute smash. Everyone's talking about it.'

'I'm so excited for it, such a novel way of going about things to just make a call on Christmas Eve and you either go straight for an audition or miss out.'

23

Linzi Carlisle

'Gerard's in, Lucy and Adrian too - he's the male lead, oh, and Bianca's the female lead, lucky thing. Of course, no one's supposed to breathe a word about it.'

'It opens New Year's Day I believe – perfect to have something to look forward to after all the parties. Stuart's furious that he ignored the phone call, poor love...'

Their voices disappeared into the music as the door opened again, and Helen opened the door, washing her hands and looking into the mirror. Why hadn't she received a call?

Alex pounced on her as she reappeared, 'Darling, you're not terribly upset with Bianca, are you? You know what a cut throat business it is, everyone out for themselves and all that.'

'Did Serena call you, Alex?' she watched his eyes.

'Why yes, of course, angel, she called all of us. I was surprised that you didn't audition, but Bianca said that you wanted to catch up on your beauty sleep, Heaven knows I should have been doing that.'

She needed to speak to Serena, maybe there were still some roles available. Easing her way through the jumble of bodies, she finally found her surrounded by a sycophantic crowd of actors fawning over her every word.

'Helen, dearest, so sorry that you missed my call, I had the most marvellous role for you, but Bianca turned out to be quite perfect. You'll still come to the show, won't you?'

'Yes, of course, if only I'd known that you called, I would have come straight down.'

'Didn't Bianca tell you? She said that you were desperate for sleep, and don't I know that feeling. But, my darling, we never sleep in this business.' She turned away as her name was called, and Helen walked slowly off.

Bianca had betrayed her. They always shared audition information, pleased for each other if one of them was cast.

She found Bianca at the bar. 'When were you going to tell me?'

'Oh, Hels, come here and give me a hug, I feel so dreadful, I really do, but I really needed this role, I have literally no money in my account. And you were so fast asleep, you'd never have been able to get ready in time, I literally had to fly out of the door. I was going to tell you after the party. Forgive me?' Fluttering her eyelashes, she pulled her mouth into a moue, 'Here, have some champagne.' She passed a glass to Helen, smiling sweetly, 'Say you don't hate me, I couldn't bear it.'

'I don't hate you,' Helen walked off disconsolately, looking around her as she walked to the front door. What a shallow bunch of people they were, all out for their own ends. But wasn't she the same? Would she have woken Bianca if she'd been the one to take the call from Serena? Well, yes, she would actually, she answered herself. She could never have treated her friend and flatmate like that.

Back home in her flat, Helen took off her dress and pulled on warm pyjamas. Stupid dress, it had cost her eighty-five pounds, which she could ill afford, and now she had the lunch at Salvatore's tomorrow, which would probably cost her about two hundred pounds once they included drinks. And she had no money coming in for the next week or two. For a moment she considered phoning her mum, but what could she say to her? Oh, Mum, I'm spending fortunes of money that I don't have and I missed out on an audition today because I was sleeping off the effects of too much champagne from another party. No, she couldn't call her, besides, it was too late, her parents were probably tucked up in bed asleep by now, having an early night.

'This was nice, wasn't it?' smiling, Mary looked around the table as everyone finished their food. 'There's no pudding, I'm afraid, I didn't even think of it.'

'Not surprising, all the toing and froing from the convenience store with your arms loaded up with pizzas and things,' Archie smiled across at his wife. 'Tell you what, Jeff, how about we open another bottle of that wine? My wife can tell us what we're eating tomorrow, it's the strangest assortment of grub that I've ever seen.'

'Aren't we going to Uncle Richard's tomorrow? Mum said we probably were.'

'No, dear, we're staying here, your Uncle Richard's off in Thailand with Sandy. I expect they're having a wonderful time in the sun.'

'Well, where's the turkey then?' Matthew screwed his face up in confusion.

'No turkey, no Christmas dinner for us,' Archie and his wife exchanged glances as Matthew's face fell, 'but your grandma's got eggs and bacon lined up for breakfast and, what are having exactly for dinner?'

'Chicken pie and pizza, frozen chips-' Mary giggled, it did sound quite mad.

'Frozen chips? For Christmas dinner?' Michaela's face was aghast, she'd been planning a selfie for her Instagram account, in front of a prettily laid up Christmas dinner table.

Skipping Christmas in Holly Crescent

'It's not Christmas dinner, Grandad just said, and I love frozen chips. Will there be more garlic bread to go with the pizza, grandma?' Matthew grinned. 'I think it all sounds kind of cool.'

'That's the spirit, son,' Archie reached over and patted his grandson's arm, 'haven't we got some ice cream in the freezer, love?'

'I forgot about that, yes, who wants some?'

'I could knock up a few pancakes to go with it if you like?'

'Pancakes and ice cream, two of my favourite things,' Matthew nudged his sister, 'you like them too, Micky, don't pretend you don't.'

'Are you sure, Jeff? That sounds delicious.'

'Totally sure, I used to be a bit of a dab hand in the kitchen. I'll clear these plates and get started.'

'We'll have to have them in front of the tele, the film's coming on in fifteen minutes.'

Everyone rushed around, clearing the table, washing up the dinner plates, and passing Jeff ingredients as he called them out, laughing as he flipped the first pancake unsuccessfully and applauding loudly as the next one flipped perfectly.

Mary looked around happily a short while later as they all sat, replete from their pancakes and ice cream, their eyes glued to the Agatha Christie film. What a perfectly enjoyable evening it had turned out to be. She reached over and patted Jeff's arm, 'I'm so pleased you're staying with us.'

'Me too, more than you know' Jeff smiled back, feeling thankful for the kindness shown to him, shuddering inwardly at the thought of having had to have spent another night out in the cold and rain, sleeping in a bus shelter.

'That was a brilliant film,' I'd never have guessed the ending,' Matthew yawned, tiredness coming over him.

'It was great, and Johnny Depp was brilliant,' Michaela agreed.

'It was very enjoyable. Of course, the book was better, even if was written decades ago, but that's Agatha Christie for you, the Queen of Crime. We've got all her books up in the attic, they were your grandma's when she was a young girl, perhaps you'd like to read some of them, get that imagination going,' Archie enthused.

'Someone wrote a book from the film? But if they're old, then how comes Johnny Depp was already in the film?' Michaela looked at her grandma, mystified.

'The books all came first, love, but that's the thing about Agatha Christie, her stories are so good that some of them have had a number of films made of them, and some for television, of course, like the Poirot series. I think she must have written that one about eighty or so years ago, certainly before I was born, but I remember reading it and finding it so exciting.'

'But that's ancient.'

'Careful, we're getting close to ancient over here,' Archie winked at his wife.

'Right, I think it's bed for you two,' Mary spoke after checking her watch.

Once the children were in bed, Mary put the kettle on and made the three of them a cup of tea before they all turned in for the night.

'I'd like to explain to you why I was in prison, if you don't mind,' Jeff leaned forward, his eyes anxious.

Archie glanced at his wife, 'You don't have to Jeff, we don't want you to feel uncomfortable.'

'I'd like to, you've both been so trusting.' At their nod, he leaned back and began to speak.

'My wife's name is Fran, well my ex-wife now, and my son's name is Luke, he's fourteen. Things were tight financially, I was trying to support the family on my own after Fran lost her part-time job. I worked as a chef for a small restaurant – nothing fancy, just casual dining – but the restaurant closed and I was struggling to find work so we were living on emergency savings I'd managed to put by. Life wasn't much fun, there was nothing to spare for luxuries, no holidays, but I figured we could pay our way for a few months while I found work,' he smiled grimly.

'Then I found out that Fran was having an affair and had been taking money from the account. It turns out she was in love with him and the next thing I knew she'd moved out and taken Luke with her, as well as the rest of the money in the account. The landlord told me I had to get out of the flat if I couldn't pay. I can't blame him, it wasn't his fault, so the day before I had to leave, I drank the contents of our booze cabinet – it wasn't even that much, some whisky, a little vodka, the remains of a bottle of Ouzo brought back from Greece in happier times, and some cheap wine, it was the mixture I suppose.'

He held his hands out as he looked at them both, 'I'm not even a big drinker, I just downed the lot, drowning my sorrows, I suppose. But then I became angry, especially with Fran and her new chap, angry with her for cheating, angry with her for taking the money, angry with her for taking my son, but most of all just angry with her for being alright when I wasn't. I walked to the house she was living in - a nice little detached house, pretty garden, decent car parked in the drive, and I saw red.'

Archie and Mary nodded encouragingly, sensing his discomfiture.

'I started drunkenly ripping the plants out of the garden, shouting at the house like a madman, and then I picked up a heavy flower urn and threw it at the car. The driver's window smashed and it felt so good, I picked it up and threw it again. Fran opened the front door and yelled at me, so I picked up another garden ornament and threw it at the front window. It smashed, of course, and I suddenly realised that my son could be in there, that I could have hurt him, and I just collapsed on the lawn. The cops came and took me away and the rest is history – three months in prison for property damage. Luke was fine, he was at school, and I'm grateful to this day that he didn't witness my meltdown in action.'

Taking in Jeff's distraught face, Mary moved beside him, taking him in her arms, 'You need a hug.'

Archie cleared his throat, 'Thank you for telling us, Jeff, I know that can't have been easy. We all know what you did wasn't right, but you've paid your dues, and I must say that I don't blame you for reacting the way you did, you took some hard knocks, one after the other, no wonder it drove you over the edge. But you'll be alright now, you'll get yourself back on your feet gradually, you'll see.'

'I hope so, thanks for listening,' Jeff smiled as Mary moved back to her armchair, 'it's such a relief to have spoken about it all, but I'll never rid myself of the feeling of shame, and you probably think I'm quite despicable.'

'I think your ex-wife's despicable,' Mary voiced what she and Archie were both feeling.

'Goodness, look at the time, it's almost midnight, we should all get ourselves off to bed, what do you say?' Archie stood up, picking up tea mugs, 'Tomorrow's another day and by all accounts it's going to be a busy one.'

Settled in their bed, Archie kissed his wife goodnight and switched off his bedside light, yawning as he closed his eyes, 'I forgot to tell you, Dulcie's brother had a fall on the ice up in Scotland and they had to cancel their visit, so she and Andrew are on their own, such a shame. Poor Dulcie's upset, Andrew said, expect he is too,' Archie nestled his head into the pillow drowsily.

Mary switched her light back on, sitting straight up in bed, 'Why ever didn't you tell me? Oh, the poor dears, all on their own. And she'd gone to so much trouble what with that pretty tree in the window, oh, and all their shopping that arrived, they must have been so looking forward to it,' she began ticking off things on her fingers.

'What are you doing?'

'Why, I'm working out what food we've got for tomorrow, they'll have to come to us, we can't have them on their own, not on-'

'Not on what? Christmas Day? Is that what you were going to say?'

'Well, yes, it won't be very festive here, we're still giving Christmas a miss, but we can make sure that no one's lonely, can't we?'

'Whatever you say, dear,' Archie began to drift off, 'but you mustn't bully them into coming.'

'Of course I won't,' snuggling back down, Mary began a mental count of their chairs and plates, falling asleep as she began to count the cutlery.

Richard breathed a sigh of relief as he fastened his seatbelt, he'd done it, he'd left his wife. Not only that, he'd left her in a hotel in Thailand - that had to be a first. Earlier in the evening he'd begun to feel guilty about his plan and had almost changed his mind, but Sandy had made sure that he remained steadfast to his plan.

She'd mocked the hotel's attempts at a Christmas Eve buffet, even going so far as to throw – to actually throw – a chicken drumstick at the hapless chef standing smiling behind the long table. She'd informed Richard that they'd better be moving to a top hotel and that it had better be a suite, at the very least. He'd told her that it was a surprise, and she'd sniffed, telling him that if he thought it would be enough to make up for his failings, he was sorely mistaken. Sloshing the plastic cup of cheap wine in his face, she'd announced that this was the last night that she'd ever drink such disgusting vinegar, but had proceeded, nonetheless, to imbibe a further five or six cups of the stuff, her face growing uglier, in his eyes, with every cup.

Well, she was certainly in for a surprise when she woke up in the morning, he smiled to himself grimly as the plane taxied for take-off, picturing her when she found the note that he'd scrawled and placed beside her as she snored loudly, before tiptoeing from the room with his suitcase.

Christmas Day

Tracy Miller woke up, scooping up the little puppy and smothering him with kisses before pulling on some tracksuit pants and a sweatshirt and taking him downstairs and out into the communal garden so that he could do his business. Back in her flat, she gave him his breakfast and took a shower, feeling excited about the day ahead. It would be so nice to spend Christmas Day with her new friends, but what was she going to do about the puppy? Anxiety crept through her as she recalled the landlord's stern speech that he'd given her when she'd returned home from her walk with Nigel.

'Absolutely no pets allowed, you agreed to that when you moved in, Miss Miller. I can't make allowances, that's not how it works. No, I'm sorry, it will have to go, I don't care what you do with it, but it goes by tomorrow, and that's an order.'

Her pleas that she was only fostering him over Christmas had fallen on deaf ears and she'd spent the rest of the evening worrying about everything. And now it was Christmas Day and she had no solution to the problem. At least she had some new friends to talk it all over with, she thought, feeling a little better, perhaps one of them would come up with a suggestion.

Susan Chavers forced one eye open, wondering where she was for a moment. Okay, she was at home, but how did she get here? She couldn't remember anything past arriving at Trevor's boss's house the day before. Oh, wait, it was slowly coming back to her, she'd drunk some Champagne, no Prosecco, and then... she couldn't find Trevor, had drunk some more, she'd even been quite amusing, hadn't she, as she'd chatted to a few of the other guests? Trevor had upset her, she'd seen the way he looked at that Pam woman, and then... she scratched furiously at her arms, opening her other eye. She was fully dressed, that wasn't good. The smell of her own stale sweat hit her and she wrinkled her nose in distaste as she remembered using the bathroom at the party and washing under her arms because- oh no, she sat up, looking at her arms in horror.

The angry rash spread almost to her elbows. She'd forgotten to apply deodorant in her rush to get ready and leave for the party, and, yes, she remembered now, she'd used the air freshener from their host's bathroom to spray under her arms. How could she have been so stupid? She'd obviously had an allergic reaction. Desperately trying to avoid the urge to scratch, she clambered out of bed and, ignoring the giddiness, stumbled down the stairs, calling out Trevor's name.

The house was silent. Where was he? A piece of folded paper on top of his laptop on the dining room table caught her eye and she approached it warily, spying her name scrawled on it.

Open my laptop and look at the page that's open. I've gone to see my parents to explain that we won't be having Christmas Day lunch with them. We need to talk when I get back, there's something I should have told you.

What? What had happened? A chill spread through her at his words. We need to talk. It sounded so ominous. Fearfully, she opened the laptop, scaring at the screen in horror.

Slowly, she clicked on each photo, moaning in humiliation as she looked at the apparition so perfectly captured by the enthusiastic photographer.

There she was, in a gold sequinned dress, which barely covered her thighs, appearing through the parted curtains, a bewildered look on her face as she grinned wildly out at what had presumably been an audience. Her arms were spread out, giving a prefect view of the angry red rash running from her underarms down towards her elbows. Caught mid-step, her arms appeared to flail helplessly as she pitched forward onto some kind of stage. Prone, her red, rash-covered arms outspread, she lay flat on her face, the dress open at the back revealing her bra strap and, horror of horrors, for the final indignity of all, her knickers were revealed in all their glory as they encompassed not only her buttocks but also the dress, which was tucked into them at the back.

Miserably she read the caption - Christmas Eve Freak Show – tears forming in her eyes and running down her cheeks. She closed the laptop and stood up, climbing the stairs slowly and throwing herself on the bed in despair.

She remembered it all now, the stupid fashion show fun, how she'd enthusiastically agreed to participate - all thanks to the prosecco and an empty stomach, and an absence of Trevor. She could never live this down.

She'd ruined everything. She was the laughing stock of his colleagues and he'd never forgive her. She never wanted to see any of those people again, ever, and knew, without a doubt, that Trevor never wanted to see her again, apart from to tell her that it was over.

Standing, she removed her clothing and stepped under the shower, enjoying the torture of the freezing water before it warmed up. Sobbing, she washed her hair, before gently soaping her body, wincing as the soap stung her rash. Wrapped in a towel, she hunted frantically through the bathroom cabinet, almost crying with relief when she found the calamine lotion.

Oh, it felt good, so good... she flung herself back on the bed, her arms out, allowing the soothing calamine lotion to take effect. Some Christmas this was turning out to be. An image of her children came into her mind and, shamefully, she realised that she hadn't even thought of them, she'd been so wrapped up in the whole her and Trevor thing. Her poor children, farmed off to their grandparents without a word and either stuck there all day or, just as dreadful for them, off to spend the day at her brother Richard's with his money-grabbing trophy wife.

Suddenly she saw herself, her stupid selfish self, not thinking of anyone else except herself, especially her parents, whom she just took for granted. She hadn't once asked them what their Christmas plans were, hadn't even been to see them for weeks, hadn't even replied to her mum's last few messages, so wrapped up had she been in her new relationship with Trevor, who they hadn't even met. Well, they wouldn't be meeting him now, would they?

Suddenly, Susan was filled with an overwhelming desire to see her mum, to be given a cuddle and a cup of tea, and to immerse herself in the sounds of her mum's gentle chatter. Guilt consumed her as she recalled the last time she'd seen her parents, when they'd called in one day at an inconvenient moment, which she'd made abundantly clear to them. She forced herself to picture her dear dad's slightly bewildered expression as he'd nodded understandingly and made a show of looking at his watch before announcing that they had best be going anyway, and her mum's attempt at hiding her hurt after Susan had all but snapped at her to leave the kitchen alone and stop interfering.

She was the worst daughter in the world. And for her pièce de résistance, she'd sent her unwanted kids there yesterday, in a taxi, and had simply informed her mother via a text message that they'd be staying with them for a couple of nights. And all because she was so desperately trying to keep up with Trevor's world – a world of youth and beauty – which she clearly had no place in.

And even after all that, her caring mum had called her yesterday, out of concern, to tell her that she was worried about her, and what had Susan done? Snapped at her, been short, dismissed her as least important in the pecking order of things - for clearly the most important thing in her life at that moment had been finding an outfit to wear to Trevor's boss's stupid party. She hadn't even thanked her mum for looking after the kids for her.

Standing up from the bed, she looked at herself in the mirror, at her despicable, terrible self, for a moment, before grabbing some toilet paper and blowing her nose. She'd go to her parents - even if they were going to Richard's for lunch they wouldn't be leaving until later - and she'd tell them how sorry she was. She'd make things right with them, she'd collect her children and bring them home for Christmas Day, and when Trevor returned to collect his things and inform her that he was moving out, she'd be calm and display absolutely no desperation, and in so doing, attempt to claw back just a little of the dignity that she'd so spectacularly lost the evening before.

Christmas Day. Fabulous. Helen clambered out of bed, wrapping the duvet around her, and walked to the window to look at the gloomy, cloud-filled sky. It looked as bleak as she felt. The last thing in the world that she felt like doing was going to Salvatore's for lunch with everyone. To do what? To share in everyone's excitement as they talked about Serena's new production and when rehearsals began? To celebrate Bianca's lead role in the pop-up stage play, which she'd got by her underhand action? Oh, stop it, Helen, she remonstrated with herself, maybe Bianca would have got the part anyway, even if Helen had auditioned.

And what did it all matter? There'd be other roles, she'd just have to take whatever casual work she could find and keep trying. But she had to stop wasting money, especially on social occasions organised by Alex with all his money to burn. She picked up her phone and sent him a short text to say that she couldn't make it after all, throwing in, as an afterthought, that she'd decided to spend the day with the parents.

The excuse brought up uncomfortable feelings of guilt and she scrolled back through her phone to see when she'd last communicated with her mother. Ah, not so long ago, just the day before yesterday when she'd apologised for not being able to pop in after all. Except she hadn't been supposed to just pop in, her eyes scanned the previous messages in the thread, she'd been supposed to be going there for dinner. There it was, quite clearly, an invitation to dinner for seven o'clock, her confirmation, and her mum's message saying how much they were looking forward to seeing her. She'd make her special homemade chicken pie for the occasion.

Shame washed over her as she read her dismissive message saying that she couldn't pop in after all, that there was an important party, and that she sent kisses. Kisses in a text message – like that made everything alright. Her mum must have realised that she'd totally forgotten that she was supposed to be having dinner with them. She felt her face flush with remorse as she imagined her mum reading the text from her selfish daughter, and then taking the pie out of the oven, the two of them sitting quietly at the table eating their dinner in disappointment. The image made her feel so sad and tears pricked her eyes.

She needed to go and see them. Today. But she didn't need to, she wanted to, she realised, her spirits lifting. She wanted to walk into their unpretentious little house, to hug them both close, to tell them how sorry she was for her selfish behaviour, to wish them a Happy Christmas, and to sit in the kitchen eating a plate of her mum's eggs and bacon with a cup of tea from her dad. They were probably sitting there all on their own and would enjoy the surprise. At least... more guilt... she actually had no idea what they'd got planned for the day, having been too wrapped up in her own life to even ask them, so she'd just take a chance.

Humming, she walked through to the kitchen and put the kettle on, her stomach rumbling in hunger. There had to be something other than rice cakes to eat in this kitchen, surely. A search of the cupboards brought forth half a packet of stale biscuits, but she hit the jackpot in the freezer, triumphantly lifting out the frost-filled bag containing the remains of a loaf of bread.

With black teas – why did they always forget to buy milk? – and a plate of dry toast spread with marmite, she pushed Bianca's door open, placing the tray on the bed and opening the curtains. 'Happy Christmas, darling, I've made you breakfast in bed.'

'Oh, you absolute angel,' Bianca's mop of tousled hair appeared from beneath the duvet. 'Happy Christmas, sweetie. What happened to you last night, you disappeared? I feel dreadful, are you still upset with me?'

Helen munched on the toast, her eyes closing in bliss. 'This tastes so good, when did we last have toast for breakfast? It would have been even nicer with some butter on it though, wouldn't it? I'm not upset with you, what's the point? You did what you felt you had to do to get the part and you got it. I missed out but maybe if I hadn't been sleeping after a night of partying, I'd have got to audition too.'

'Thank you for being kind,' Bianca's face broke into a relieved smile, 'and now we have to get ready for Salvatore's, it's going to be magnificent, what are you wearing?'

'I'm not going,' Helen put her empty plate down, 'I'm going to see my mum and dad, I haven't treated them very well lately, to my shame.'

'But you can see them any day,' Bianca pleaded.

'No, that's just it, there'll always be something, some party or lunch that we absolutely must go to, must be seen at in the hopes of catching the eye of some producer. But I realised that any day just conveniently never comes, I need to make a choice, and today I choose to see my mum and dad, to wish them a Happy Christmas and,' she grinned, 'to eat some of my mum's fried eggs and to eat toast with butter on it.'

'That actually sounds so good,' Bianca laughed.

Mary awoke early, taking advantage of the sleeping household to have her shower and get dressed, before heading downstairs and opening the curtains. The grey, cloud-filled sky did nothing to dampen her spirits, today was going to be a wonderful day, she thought happily - a wonderful day of not doing the whole Christmas thing but of filling their home with friends and neighbours, to talk, to laugh, to eat cobbled together meals, and to bring each other much-needed company. She made a big pot of tea, laying out mugs and a plate of her homemade biscuits beside it, switched the oven on and laid out some of her sausage rolls on a tray before sliding them into the oven to warm gently, and poured herself a cup as she heard the sounds of wakening from upstairs.

Slipping out of the house, she walked next door to number ten, noting the light on in the front room. She knocked on the door.

'Good morning, Mary, a Happy Christmas to you,' Andrew Hope smiled in surprise.

'And to you, Andrew, er, may I come in for a moment?'

Dulcie looked up, blowing her nose and wiping her eyes. It was silly to be feeling so upset about everything, but the day ahead just felt so bleak. She tried to smile as Mary walked into the living room.

'Oh, Dulcie,' Mary sat down next to the elderly woman, wrapping her arms around her, 'Archie told me about Alasdair, I'm so sorry, what a worry for you, and all your plans spoiled.'

Nodding, Dulcie blew her nose again, 'Silly to be getting so upset. It's just that we were really looking forward to the company, I'd even bought pigs in blankets. And Archie got a real tree, look at the stupid thing with all its ribbons and lights, oh dear,' she sniffed, wiping her eyes again.

Squeezing Dulcie's shoulders, Mary smiled as she spoke, 'Well, I've got a favour to ask you, and I do hope you'll both say yes, you'd be really helping us out.'

'Always pleased to help, aren't we, dear?' Andrew nodded encouragingly at his wife and they both looked at Mary, 'what do you need?'

'Well, your company actually - for the whole day, starting right now. I've got a fresh pot of tea next door, homemade biscuits, sausage rolls warming in the oven, and the most ridiculous dinner lined up for later. We decided to skip Christmas this year, with all our children busy, and save ourselves the bother of all that tiring shopping in the crowds and putting up decorations,' she grinned at them, 'but we seem to have ended up with a few wonderful waifs and strays joining us in our home nonetheless, including our grandchildren, and I just know that everyone would love to have you join us. Please say yes.'

'That sounds marvellous.'

'Are you sure, we wouldn't want to be a bother?'

They both spoke at once.

'I've never been more sure about anything, so it's decided then, there's just one thing...'

'Name it.'

'We'll need to borrow your dining chairs if you don't mind, and perhaps your table too...'

Andrew laughed, 'Certainly, if you've got the young men to fetch them.'

'And we've got a gammon in the fridge, I soaked it overnight so it just needs cooking, and we could bring pigs in blankets,' Dulcie's eyes sparkled.

'And the cake, don't forget the Christmas cake.'

'And all that wine that we bought.'

'We're going to have a feast beyond compare, it will all go perfectly with my homemade chicken pie, and the pizzas and chips from the convenience store,' chuckling in amusement, Mary stood up, 'I'll let you get yourselves ready and I'll send Archie and Jeff round to fetch the table and chairs, and my grandson too, if he's out of bed yet.'

'Thank you, Mary,' Dulcie hugged her tightly, 'you're a kind woman and you've cheered us both up so much.'

'Now don't take too long, I'll be cooking a full English breakfast for us all just as soon as everyone arrives.'

'I'm on my way,' Andrew joked, 'nothing beats a plate of eggs and bacon.'

Matthew was talking animatedly to Jeff about the plot of the film they'd watched the night before, a sausage roll in one hand, biscuit in the other, taking alternate bites from each, much to Jeff's amusement.

They looked up as Mary walked into the kitchen.

'These biscuits are the best, Grandma, and these sausage rolls, aren't they, Jeff? You're the best cook ever.'

'Don't eat too many, you'll spoil your breakfast,' she flushed happily as she kissed her husband on the cheek.

'Now, I need you men to head next door to bring the dining chairs and table round, Andrew and Dulcie are joining us for the day.'

'More people? This is like a proper Christmas Day,' Matthew grabbed another sausage roll, laughing as his grandma tapped his hand.

The doorbell rang and Jeff hurried to open it, his face breaking into a smile, 'Come in, everyone, nice to see you all. And you,' he reached out and stroked the puppy's head, 'what's your name?'

'He doesn't have a name, I'm fostering him, well, I was. I'm Tracy by the way, sorry.'

'Jeff, pleased to meet you, Tracy, and the puppy with no name.' He stood back, waving them in from the cold. 'Nigel, good to see you again, mate, oh, and Happy Christmas, everyone.' He smiled at Joan, 'Hello again, Joan, you look nice.'

'Thank you, too, Jeff,' Joan blushed. 'Are we supposed to be saying Happy Christmas? I thought Mary said we were ignoring it.'

'Well, if we're ignoring it then she and Archie have got a funny way of going about it, it certainly feels like Christmas to me.'

Joan handed him a large bag, 'We stopped at the shop and collected the leftover boxes of Christmas crackers, but I'm not sure if-'

Skipping Christmas in Holly Crescent

Jeff winked, 'Brilliant idea, tell you what, I'll hide them in my room until we see how the land lies, then we can get them out a bit later for the dinner table, how's that?'

Mary rushed through, hugging everyone in welcome, 'You can pop your coats upstairs in our bedroom, then come on into the kitchen for some tea and biscuits. There are sausage rolls too. Oh, and Nigel, perhaps you could help the men carry the chairs round from next door? This is Archie, my husband, this is Matthew, my grandson, and this is Tracy, and the dear puppy. My granddaughter is somewhere, still asleep if I know Michaela.'

'I'm here,' Michaela descended the stairs sleepily in her pyjamas, wondering what all the noise was about.

'Here she is, my beautiful granddaughter,' announced Mary proudly, as she ran through the names of her guests again.

He was gorgeous. She felt mortified. Why hadn't her grandma told her that she'd invited an absolute hunk? She was wearing her pyjamas - and she hadn't even brushed her teeth yet. Embarrassed, Michaela smiled, keeping her lips together, before turning tail and rushing back up the stairs. She needed to shower and wash her hair and get some make-up on. And what was she going to wear?

'A bit shy, is she?' Joan nodded in understanding, 'I remember what it was like to be that age. She must be about the same age as you, Nigel.'

'Sixteen,' Archie informed Joan, 'but trust me, she's not usually so shy, I'm not sure what's come over her.'

'Here are the frozen chips, and, it's nothing special, but I collected some frozen cheesecakes from the shop as well, I thought they might come in handy for pudding,' Joan passed the carrier bag to Mary.

'Wonderful, these look delicious, thank you Joan, that's very thoughtful, I'll squeeze them in the freezer. Now, Tracy, let me have a hold of this little boy while you take your coat upstairs. Nigel, could you pop his basket in the corner in the lounge? Do you think he needs to go out in the garden at all?'

'Thanks, Mary, he might do. And thanks again for having me,' Tracy smiled shyly. Where shall I put his food bowl?'

'We'll put that in the lean to and I'll get a bowl of water put down.' Mary breathed in the puppy's smell happily as she got everyone organised. 'Help yourselves to tea and sausage rolls, and biscuits, if Matthew's left any. And Archie, you men had better get round to next door.'

Archie mock-saluted, before gathering Jeff, Matthew, and Nigel, 'Let's go, boys.'

Popping the puppy down on the grass, Mary folded her arms against the cold, glancing up at the sky. It was the most miserable weather and yet it was turning out to be the most wonderful day, and it was only just beginning. She hugged herself happily, praising the puppy as he lifted his little leg, before scooping him back up and heading back indoors. Tracy had seemed a little anxious, but maybe that was just the way she was, nonetheless, she'd keep an eye on her, she didn't want anyone to feel anything but happy today.

Matthew and Nigel ran back and forth, ferrying the ham and other food items, as Mary received them, while frying sausages and bacon. Joan and Tracy were charged with re-organising the lounge furniture to better accommodate the extra dining table and chairs, and a short while later Jeff brought in the last two chairs from Andrew and Dulcie's house.

'Are you sure ten chairs are going to be enough, Mary?' he joked, 'Any more guests likely to appear?'

She flapped him away, laughing, as she laid two mismatched table cloths on the adjoining tables, topping them with placemats.

A couple of minutes later a bustle at the front door made her look up, and she beamed, opening her arms to embrace Andrew and Dulcie. 'Come in and meet everyone, let me take your coats, come into the lounge in the warm.'

Mary stared out of the lounge window in surprise as a fully decorated Christmas tree made its way down the path to the front door.

'What do you think? Dulcie suggested it, and it seemed a shame for it to sit there in their front room all alone.' Archie shrugged, as Matthew looked at her hopefully.

'Well, it is lovely, and at least this way everyone gets to enjoy it. Besides, you've carried it round now, and it will cheer up Andrew and Dulcie. If you put it in the bay window, you'll be able to plug the lights in. It will look nice and-'

'Festive?' suggested Archie, grinning.

'Like Christmas?' Jeff winked at her.

'Like a brilliant Christmas,' Matthew enthused, as he sniffed the air. 'When are we having breakfast? I'm starving. My Grandma's a brilliant cook,' he informed his new friend, Nigel.

Linzi Carlisle

'I've just got to do the eggs and toast the muffins, so you can put the knives and forks out. Oh, I forgot about orange juice, we haven't got any.'

'Nigel can fetch some from the shop, why don't you take Matthew with you?' Joan rummaged in her bag, passing her son the keys, 'Don't forget to lock up afterwards.'

'It must be really cool having a mum who owns a shop,' Matthew looked around at all the shelves as they picked up cartons of fruit juice.

'It's alright, she works hard though, and she's always tired because she has to work so late.'

'Can't she get someone to help her?'

'Well, she could, but she said she can't do that until she can afford it, maybe in another year or two.'

'Why did your sister run back upstairs? Is she really shy or something?' The two boys walked slowly back as they chatted.

'She's not normally shy, she's usually full of herself, and she's really bossy, and always moaning about everything. Did you see the Agatha Christie film last night? About the murder on the train?'

'I've read the book, but Mum wanted to watch something else last night, some kind of Christmas romance film, you know, where the woman's lonely and then she meets some guy who's new in town and who comes into her life unexpectedly and then they fall in love as it starts to snow.'

Matthew scoffed, 'Those things are so farfetched, like it ever happens in real life. We've got the orange juice,' he yelled, as they walked in.

'Perfect timing, thanks, boys, I'm just about to serve up. Go and wash your hands, and Tracy, could you pop these on the table for me?'

'Have you seen the puppy?' Nigel asked Matthew, 'he's really cute.'

A waft of perfume heralded Michaela's second appearance, this time in her dusky grey leggings, grey slipper boots, and pale pink jumper, together with a perfectly made-up face.

'You look pretty, darling,' Mary smiled at her granddaughter, 'can you help me carry the dishes through?' Taking a last check around the kitchen, Mary felt Archie's arms encircle her waist.

'Happy, love? We've got quite the houseful for two old crocks who aren't having a Christmas this year.'

She leaned back against him for a moment, 'It's wonderful, isn't it? All so unexpected, and so much fun. I miss the kids, of course, but I expect they're all having a good time, wherever they are.'

Finally, everyone was seated and they loaded up their plates with sausages, bacon, fried eggs and buttery muffins. Everyone was talking at once, laughing, as they passed the salt and pepper back and forth, and appreciative murmurs and compliments were plentiful as they all tucked in.

'There's plenty more, I've got more eggs frying in the pan, and more bacon in the oven.'

'Smile,' Michaela took photographs of the food, the smiling faces, and the Christmas tree with its twinkling lights. It was beginning to look a lot more like Christmas, she thought happily, finally she'd have something to post on Instagram. It didn't quite go with her theme, but it would make her friends jealous when they saw Nigel. She took a selfie, making sure that he was clearly visible behind her.

A taxi pulled up outside, unnoticed, and a moment later the doorbell rang. Everyone looked at each other in surprise. 'Are you expecting anyone else?' someone asked.

Mary stood and walked out of the lounge, opening the front door.

'Helen,' she exclaimed, enfolding her daughter in her arms. 'Is everything alright, darling? Whatever's the matter?'

'Oh, Mum, I'm sorry, I've been such a terrible daughter. And you cooked a chicken pie specially and I forgot, and I let you down, like I always do, and you never complain.'

'There, there, don't be silly,' Mary patted her daughter's back soothingly as Archie appeared, wrapping his arms around both of them.

'Oh, Dad, I'm so sorry about the way I've behaved,' fresh tears spilled from Helen's eyes, 'I've been so selfish, so wrapped up in myself, and I didn't even think to find out if you were all alone for Christmas. But you're not,' she wiped her eyes, suddenly catching sight of the group gathered around the table through the lounge doorway. 'I've been selfish again, turning up here without even thinking that you might have plans.'

'Now come on, love, wipe your eyes, you turning up is a wonderful surprise for us both.'

'It certainly is,' Mary nodded, stroking Helen's back, 'pop upstairs and give your face a wash and then come in and meet everyone. We're having brunch and there's plenty left, I'll dish you up a nice plate of bacon and eggs, that is, if you want that, otherwise I could make you an egg white omelette?'

'Bacon and eggs sound perfect,' Helen smiled, 'I'm starving, and I'm finished with egg white omelettes and constant diets. Are Richard and Susan here? Did I just see Michaela?'

Skipping Christmas in Holly Crescent

'Your brother's off in Thailand for Christmas, with Sandy, and your sister's got her new boyfriend so I expect they're having a special first Christmas together. We've ended up with the grandchildren, it's a long story,' Mary smiled as the puppy sleepily wandered through to check on the new visitor, much to Helen's surprise, 'and this little bundle of love is another story, but go and freshen up now and then we can tell you all about it.'

'Everyone, meet our beautiful daughter, Helen,' Mary smiled proudly as she carried out the introductions, 'Helen's an actress. Here, you sit here, love, Archie, what about one of the old chairs from the lean to?'

'I'll grab one, you take my chair,' Archie hurried off.

'Mmm, these eggs are delicious, Mum, and this sausage tastes so good, I don't remember when I last ate a sausage.'

'Why not?' Matthew looked at his aunt, mystified, 'what's wrong with sausages? I love sausages.'

'Is there anything that you don't like, Matthew?' Jeff laughed in amusement.

'Um, I don't think so, no wait, Brussels sprouts, I don't like those. I don't see why we always have to have them with Christmas dinner.' His face fell, 'We haven't got them today have we, Grandma?'

'Not a Brussels sprout in sight, no, we're having a dinner with a difference this year, we're having-'

'Frozen chips,' Michaela announced, grinning.

'And pizza,' Joan added.

'Don't forget the gammon' Dulcie said, as Mary exclaimed that she should get it boiling.

'Or the pigs in blankets,' threw in Andrew, laughing.

'And your grandma's homemade chicken pie,' Archie smiled at his daughter, 'so you get to have it with us after all.'

'I think it sounds like the best Christmas Dinner ever,' Matthew beamed happily, all my favourite foods. And you forgot to say garlic bread.'

'I think I've walked into a complete madhouse,' Helen laughed, her pretty face lighting up, 'but filled with the best bunch of people, this is so much fun, thank you for letting me join you all.'

'Thank you for being here, love, the more the merrier seems to be your mother's theme of the day,' Archie beamed as everyone laughed.

Jeff smiled as he watched Archie put his arm around his daughter's shoulders, he and Mary clearly loved her so much. He was pleased that they had at least one of their children with them for Christmas Day in the end.

Joan glanced at Jeff as he looked smilingly along the table to where Helen sat next to Archie, well no surprise, she was very beautiful, and slim, with lovely hair, no wonder he couldn't keep his eyes off her. Her heart sank a little, and she reached up a hand to self-consciously tuck a strand of hair behind her ear, before leaning over and kissing Nigel on the top of his head for comfort. What had she been thinking? That she'd be given a second chance at love, like in one of those Hallmark films she liked to watch? Stupid to dream - as if a tall, dark, handsome stranger would walk into her drab little convenience store one day and sweep the lonely widow off her feet. A touch on her arm made her look up. Jeff winked at her, with a little smile, and her heart did a small flip as it rose again.

Nigel blushed as his mum kissed him on the head, she did it all the time and he didn't mind normally, but Michaela had seen and now he felt a bit embarrassed for some reason. The puppy appeared beside his chair, nuzzling his leg, and he reached down to stroke it.

'Is that a puppy?' Michaela's eyes widened in surprise as she pushed her chair back, 'where did it come from?'

Archie laughed, 'He's been sleeping here the whole time, love, while you were busy making yourself beautiful.'

'Oh, stop teasing, Archie, our granddaughter is always beautiful. Perhaps he needs to go out again,' Mary smiled, nodding to Nigel, 'why don't you youngsters take him into the garden?'

'Tracy's fostering him,' Nigel explained to Michaela as he picked up the puppy and stood up.

'He's gorgeous,' reaching to stroke the puppy, Michaela's hair brushed against Nigel's face. She smelled wonderful and his stomach did a funny kind of flip as she looked up at him.

'What's his name?'

Momentarily tongue-tied, Nigel looked at his mum helplessly.

'We really should give him a name,' Joan helped him out, 'what d'you think, Tracy, any ideas?'

Linzi Carlisle

There was that worried look again. Mary stood up, collecting some of the plates. 'Tracy, could you help me to clear the table, love?'

She turned to the young woman as she brought more plates through, 'Now, you're worried about something, darling, is it about the puppy? What's the matter?' She smiled encouragingly and Tracy looked at her anxiously.

'The thing is, my landlord saw the puppy when I got home yesterday and told me he had to go by today and I don't know what to do.'

'Well, you stop worrying right now, okay? We're all in this together now, we're like...' she searched for the words, 'one big family. Yes, that's what we are. You leave it with me and I'll have a think about it. I've got an idea,' she smiled to herself, it was a wonderful idea...

'What's that about an idea? What's cooking in that head of yours now?' Archie appeared with more plates, a happy grin on his face. 'This is turning into such a good day, isn't it?'

'Oh, nothing for you to worry about. Just look at that gorgeous little puppy out there with the kids, isn't he adorable?'

Archie gazed out at the puppy as it played, tumbling over its own legs, 'He's a real specimen, isn't he? Make me miss our little girl. I think there's an old tennis ball in the lean to, I'll take it out for him to play with.'

'Why don't you pop the kettle on, Tracy? I expect everyone would like a cup of tea,' Mary winked at Tracy as Matthew raced past to join the fun in the garden.

Susan headed towards her parents' house, feeling as empty as the roads along which she drove. Christmas had turned into the most miserable time ever, it was so different to what she'd imagined. It was probably like that for her poor children, she thought guiltily, picturing them at her parents', feeling unwanted by their own mother, as well as their father. Well, she'd make it up to them, she'd get them home and try to rustle up something for dinner, maybe find some good films for them to watch on television. She might even have some microwave popcorn in the cupboard, that would be a bit of fun. Thinking of food made her stomach growl and she realised that she'd eaten nothing since yesterday morning. Perhaps she could make some toast when she got there. But first she needed to say sorry to her poor mum and dad, and then they'd put the kettle on and all sit in their cosy little lounge and drink tea for a while. The thought was so comforting that she felt tears well up in her eyes and she brushed them away as she looked for somewhere to park, staring at the sparkling Christmas tree in her parents' front window in surprise.

'That brunch was absolutely delicious, Mary, thank you,' Jeff leaned back, patting his stomach, before standing up and clearing the last dishes from the table, with Joan's help.

'It really was, Matthew's absolutely right, you are a brilliant cook, but you should let us do the food tonight, you've been on the go for hours,' Joan began to run hot water into the bowl for the washing up as Dulcie appeared.

'I think there's someone at your door, Mary, do you want me to answer it?'

'That's odd,' Mary frowned, 'no, you and Andrew go and sit down in the comfy chairs, Dulcie, Tracy's making us all some tea, I'll go and see who's at the door.'

Seeing her mum's smiling face as she opened the door was too much for Susan's fragile state and she erupted into tears, throwing her arms around Mary. 'Oh, Mum,' she wailed, shuddering with a release of emotions.

'Susan, what is it, love? What's happened? It's alright, your mum's here,' she held her daughter close, stroking her hair gently. What on earth was going on with her daughters today? 'Come through to the kitchen, I'll get you a cup of tea.'

Susan sniffed, pulling a damp tissue from her sleeve and wiping her nose ineffectually, 'Have you got any tissues?'

'In the kitchen,' Mary smiled encouragingly.

Shrieks of laughter came from the garden, interspersed with little yaps of excitement, and a burst of cold air rushed in as Archie and the children came back inside, the puppy running excitedly between their feet.

'Mum, what are you doing here?' Matthew skidded to a halt, looking at his mum in surprise.

'You've just missed the best breakfast ever, and last night we had pizza and Jeff made pancakes, and this is the puppy that Tracy's looking after, isn't he cute? Oh, and this is my friend, Nigel.' He finally stopped to draw breath.

Archie raised his eyebrows at his wife as she passed Susan to him, folding his arms around his daughter, 'Hello, love, what a lovely surprise. Is everything alright?'

34

Skipping Christmas in Holly Crescent

Fresh tears fell from Susan's eyes and Archie gently pushed her onto a kitchen chair, 'You're alright, everything's going to be alright, tell us what the matter is.'

'Oh, Dad, I've been so awful to you and Mum, I'm sorry, I've been so wrapped up in my life, I've been so selfish, only thinking about myself and I haven't phoned, or visited, and I've taken you for granted, and now it serves me right, I'm getting everything I deserve.'

'Mum?' Michaela stopped in the kitchen, the puppy in her arms, 'What are you doing here? Why are you crying? Where's Trevor?'

Standing up, Susan reached for her children and Tracy took the puppy from Michaela, discreetly exiting the kitchen.

'I'm sorry, my darlings, I've been a terrible mother, sending you away for Christmas when you should have been at home.'

'We don't have to leave, do we? Andrew and Dulcie are here and Andrew's going to show us how to play Bagatelle, Jeff found it in the garage, and Grandad said it's like pinball machines but before they were invented. And we've got a feast for dinner, we've got more pizza, and you'll never believe it, but Grandma's serving chips for Christmas dinner.'

'Joan brought them from the shop, and cheesecake, and Aunty Helen's here, and Nigel's going to show me the books in the attic,' Michaela joined her brother's pleas, 'and we can't leave, we're looking after the puppy.' She looked desperately at her mum, 'Say we can stay, Mum, please?'

'Who are all these people?' Susan asked in surprise as she reached for another tissue, blowing her nose noisily. 'Helen's here?'

'They're all our friends, dear, perhaps you'd like to meet them in a minute? And yes, Helen's here as well. But first tell us what's happened, and you haven't been awful, how could you be? You're our precious daughter.'

'We love you terribly, you know that,' Archie patted her shoulder.

'Nigel, come into the lounge, love,' Joan whispered, beckoning her son from where he stood uncertainly in the doorway to the lean to. 'I'll take the tea tray through and pour everyone a cup,' she murmured to Mary, who nodded, tipping her head towards Matthew and Michaela.

Jeff appeared, hovering, as Joan whispered something to him. 'Come on, kids, we've got the bagatelle board set up.'

'Suze? I thought I heard your voice?' Helen walked in, smiling, stopping as she took in her sister's red, tear-stained face. 'You look terrible, sis, what's going on?'

'Trevor's left me,' Susan burst out in a wail, 'and it's all my fault, I've ruined everything.' She sniffed and hiccupped her way through her tale of woe, 'I made such a fool of myself. I've ruined things for him at work and I know he'll never forgive me. He's probably gone to Pam, I'm sure they were having an affair, but I just made it a hundred times easier for him. The photos are everywhere, I'm a laughing stock. And my arms feel like they're on fire, do you have any calamine lotion? And I'm so hungry, I haven't eaten anything since yesterday morning, could I make some toast?'

'Right, Archie, off to the lounge to keep everyone there for a while,' Mary took charge. 'Helen, pop a couple of those sausages back in the oven to warm and put the pan on for eggs, oh, and cut and toast a muffin. Susan, up to our bedroom, let's have a look at your arms and sort you out.'

Mary gently dabbed calamine lotion on her daughter's arms as she listened to the whole sorry story of Susan's disastrous Christmas Eve and her suspicions of Trevor's infidelity, tutting in sympathy as the story unfolded. 'There,' she stood back, 'that's your arms sorted out for now, I'm sure they'll feel a lot better by tomorrow. Now, as for these people from Trevor's work, they sound like an unkind bunch if you ask me, surely one of them must have seen that you were a bit tipsy and not quite yourself? It's very cruel of them to have let you get dressed up and go out on the stage like that, and then to take photographs,' she shook her head, 'and to make them public like that, I just don't understand it, I really don't.'

'And the dress was tucked in my knickers, Mum,' Susan whispered the words in shame, 'I was laying there, flat on my face, with the dress in my knickers.'

'And where was your Trevor in all this?'

'That's the thing, I don't remember anything else, I only remember earlier, he was desperate to get Pam's attention, running after her the whole time, he's obviously crazy about her.'

'So you don't know that he's having an affair, he wouldn't be running after someone if he was already with them, would he? And he must have got you dressed back in your own clothes and got you home safely? I think you need to wait until you've heard what he has to say, love, no jumping to conclusions – if it's bad news then you'll cope with it, you're a strong woman, and your dad and I are here for you, you know that,

35

and if it's not what you think, well then, all this worrying will have been for nothing. Now, let's get downstairs before Helen ruins the eggs, she never was a very good cook, and once you've eaten something you can meet everyone.'

Roars of laughter were coming from the lounge as Matthew yelled out enthusiastically, followed by a groan.

'Who's next?' Andrew was in charge of scorekeeping, 'Nigel, your turn.'

Susan smiled at her mum as they walked into the kitchen, 'I remember us all playing that when we were kids, I can't believe you've still got it.'

'How are you getting on with the eggs? Mary cast a critical eye towards the frying pan as Helen shrugged her shoulders haplessly.

'I'm afraid it's kind of turned into an omelette, is that alright, Suze?'

She grinned at her younger sister, 'For once, I'm so hungry that I don't care how bad your cooking is.'

Once she'd eaten, and feeling much better, Susan hugged her mum, 'Thanks, Mum, and thanks for having the kids at such short notice, I should never have done that to you. I'll get the kids to collect their bits in a minute and get them out of your hair.'

Mary's face fell, 'But we're all having such a lovely time, and the kids are really enjoying themselves. It's no trouble, really it isn't, and Matthew's looking forward to his Christmas dinner of pizza and chips, he can't believe his luck. Stay, have dinner with us at least, then see how things are. We've got plenty of food, quite the concoction, and it would be so lovely to have us all together.' She looked hopefully at her daughter.

'Alright then, why not? Thanks, Mum. Funny, I had an idea that you and Dad were going to Richard's for Christmas dinner? I guess I was wrong.'

'Richard's off in Thailand with Sandy, didn't you know?'

'Thailand? Lucky old them, I had no idea. I expect they're in some swanky hotel, knowing Sandy. Are they having a nice time?'

'I'm sure they are, it must be lovely to have some winter sunshine, no doubt they'll come back with suntans and lots of stories for us.'

'You haven't heard from him?' About to moan about her brother's remissness, Susan stopped herself, 'We've all been as bad as each other, too wrapped up in our own lives to think of you and Dad. That's all going to change, I promise.'

Michaela had been hovering in the doorway, 'Mum, you're not going to make us go home, are you?'

'Come here, love, no, I'll stay for dinner, it sounds interesting, and then we'll see where we are. How's that?'

'Oh, good, we're going up in the attic now to look at the books,' Michaela hurried back to the lounge.

'Books? My daughter?' Susan raised her eyebrows in disbelief.

'I think there might be an explanation for that,' grinning, Mary beckoned her, 'Let's go and introduce you to everyone and get some tea before it's all gone, and then I must put Dulcie's gammon on to cook.'

Richard shivered as he walked through the arrivals hall at Heathrow. He should have worn something warmer, it was absolutely freezing. For a moment he thought yearningly of the sunshine he'd left behind, before turning his attention to the waiting taxi driver, giving him his address as he dropped his bags in the boot and climbed into the back seat. His phone began to ping repeatedly and he looked at the long list of messages from Sandy. Expletives didn't even begin to describe them. Shutting off his phone, he stared glumly out at the grey sky as the taxi made its way through London to his home.

The house was cold and silent, and felt as miserable as the weather, when he walked in. Sighing, he took his bags upstairs and turned on the shower before remembering that he'd turned the heating off in an attempt to save a bit of money. He turned the heating on and emptied his suitcase, throwing everything in the laundry bin, before heading downstairs and putting the kettle on. Opening the fridge, he stared dispiritedly at its contents – half a packet of ham in a Tupperware, which would need throwing, a couple of shrivelled tomatoes, a pot of brown goo bearing the label guacamole, which would also need throwing, some unopened cream cheese, and the doggy bag containing the remains of the garlic steak and dauphinoise potatoes that he and Sandy had eaten at their local restaurant the night before they left for their holiday. The butter was fine, he closed the lid again, before picking up the milk - definitely not fine.

Opening the bin, he threw everything except the cream cheese and the butter into it and took a loaf of bread from the freezer. He could always have toast for his Christmas dinner, or he could defrost something from the freezer, or get a takeaway – were they even open on Christmas day, though? Maybe the pizza places were. He thought longingly of his mum's roast turkey, roast potatoes and all the vegetable dishes she always did, sweet carrots, cauliflower cheese, Brussels sprouts, and her thick gravy to pour all over everything, an image of her laden Christmas Day dinner table coming into his mind.

He could surprise them, he decided suddenly, they were probably sitting there all on their own and would love a bit of company. No doubt Susan was tied up with her new boyfriend, it being their first Christmas together, and Helen was always out with her theatre friends partying up a storm, so they'd be really happy to see him. He'd have a bit of apologising to do, he realised, feeling guilty, he hadn't been in touch since before he'd left for the holiday, hadn't even wished them a Happy Christmas. Well, he could make up for it now, he'd take a bottle of wine from the wine rack and grab some flowers from a petrol station on his way, he might even be able to pick up a box of chocolates as well.

Feeling energised, he headed back upstairs to test the shower temperature, impatient now to get going, the thought of a roast dinner having him salivating in anticipation, as well as, he thought in surprise, the thought of seeing his dear old mum and dad. He'd take a small bag with him, perhaps he could stay the night in their spare room, it would be nice to wake up in the morning to a cup of tea from dad and the smell of mum's cooked breakfast wafting up the stairs.

Jeff pulled the ladder down, fastening it securely, and stepped back, as Archie stood at the bottom, giving instructions to his assembled group.

'Now, you'll find two big cardboard boxes over on the left, next to the green suitcase, it says 'books' on them, and the other two are over the other side, together with a box of old records. You might want to bring the boxes down, it'll get jolly cold up there if you stay there too long. And don't forget, you're welcome to any of the books, you just have to promise me one thing.'

Four pairs of eyes stared at him, waiting for him to tell them what it was.

'If you take some books then you must read them. Do we have a deal?'

Two heads nodded vigorously, one a little slower, and Matthew gaped at his grandad.

'What are records?'

Tracy giggled as Archie guffawed, tousling his grandson's hair, 'Long before your day, my boy, let's save that for another day, stick to the books for now, okay?'

Jeff grinned once the two men were left alone on the landing, 'Makes me feel old, kids not knowing what records are, or cassette tapes, or compact discs, I suppose. All the fun they missed out on, recording favourite tracks from a record, trying to stop the needle from making too much noise as you gently lowered in onto the vinyl, trying to stop the record button on the tape recorder from making too much of a clunk, which it always did. And all the cables, red and yellow, weren't they? Connecting everything to make it work, what an effort it all took.' He smiled in memory as he continued his reminiscing.

'Then there was the reverential placing of a fresh, unused, blank tape in the tape recorder, the hunched position and concentration as I'd listen to the top forty chart on Radio One on a Sunday afternoon, desperately trying to press record at exactly the right time so as not to get the DJ's voice included. It required even more skill if an old tape was being recorded over, of course, the risk of leaving fragments of old songs in between each recorded single, to ruin the precious mix tape, needed extreme concentration. Those were the days indeed.'

'They certainly were,' Archie nodded, 'everything seemed so much simpler in those days, didn't it?'

'It did, although today's kids would probably say it all sounds too complicated, especially compared to their just having to touch their phone screens and pretty much watch, listen to, or find out about, anything in the world.'

'You ask me, all that sounds a lot more complicated, beats me how they work it all out,' shaking his head, Archie headed for the stairs. 'Time for a sit down, I reckon.'

'There's a box of Christmas decorations up here,' Matthew's head appeared, hanging upside down through the attic opening, 'can we put some up?'

'It's a bit late in the day now, isn't it?' Jeff shrugged, looking at Archie.

'Well, I don't suppose it would harm, just don't go too crazy, your Grandma and I skipped Christmas completely this year to save ourselves all the fuss and bother of all that kind of stuff.'

Matthew looked baffled, 'Skipped Christmas? But you and Grandma are having Christmas, we all are, and it's a brilliant one, it's much more fun than normal, I've never had pizza for Christmas dinner before. How long is it until dinner? I'm feeling a bit hungry. I'll bring the decorations down.' His head disappeared from view.

Jeff laughed, 'I swear all that boy thinks about is food, and pizza in particular.'

The lounge was quiet, Andrew, Dulcie, and Mary, being fast asleep, and Archie lowered himself onto the sofa beside his wife, leaning back and closing his eyes contentedly. Susan and Helen were chatting quietly at the dinner table, but there was no sign of Joan. Walking quietly to the kitchen, Jeff heard a soft voice from the garden and looked out of the window, spying Joan as she praised the puppy, her arms wrapped around herself in the cold. He grabbed his thick jacket and joined her, wrapping his jacket around her shoulders.

'Thank you,' Joan breathed in his scent from the jacket, 'I didn't mean to stay out here so long, but he's having such fun with his ball.'

'Joan, could I tell you something? Something about me and where I've been?'

'You don't have to, whatever it is it doesn't matter.'

'I'd like to.'

'Then I'd like to hear it. Shall we go inside though? It's freezing.'

They sat down in the kitchen and Jeff told Joan what he'd told Archie and Mary, as she listened sympathetically, her eyes gentle through her glasses.

Tracy held up the old copy of Jane Eyre, 'Oh, this was one of my favourite stories as a young girl, I must have read it so many times. Look how beautiful this cover is, it must be really old.' She opened the book, scanning the small print inside. 'It's over a hundred years old, that's amazing.'

'It's so pretty,' Michaela reached for the book, admiring its green cloth cover and embossing, 'I love the illustration of the woman. What's it about?'

Tracy looked at her in amazement, 'You haven't read it, not even at school?'

'No,' shaking her head, Michaela listened as Tracy gave her a brief synopsis of the much-loved story.

'Look at this,' Nigel lifted out the book from the other box, 'Swallows and Amazons, I got this from the library when I was younger, it was one of my favourite books. Looks like this copy's been read quite a few times.'

'This one is so cute,' Michaela held the book, smiling at the little people in the illustration, 'The Borrowers, I wonder what that's about exactly?'

Again, Tracy was amazed, whilst inwardly conceding that she herself was an absolute bookworm, almost from birth it sometimes felt. 'It's a really sweet story, it's about little people who live underneath the floorboards, there are a few of them.'

Nigel was busy laying out the Enid Blyton books, 'Did you read the Secret Seven series, Tracy? Michaela, look, here's your grandad's name written inside. He must have had these when he was a boy.'

'And here are the Agatha Christies,' smiling, Michaela opened the cover of After the Funeral, 'oh, look, it says Mary Summerly, that was Grandma's name.'

Tracy took out her phone, laying out some of the books and taking photos of them, 'I'll ask Mary and Archie first, but some of these will be great for bookstagram. I run the library's Instagram account but I've got my personal one too.'

Michaela held up the Agatha Christie and posed for a selfie, making sure that Nigel was in the background. That would show Rachel Hounslow in her pink bobble hat.

'You'll have to read it now,' Nigel grinned at her, 'we should all follow each other, what are your accounts called?'

'Where did Matthew go?'

They looked around the attic in surprise.

'He must have got bored. Let's take some of these books downstairs and see what everyone's doing.'

'Thanks for telling me, it must have been so hard for you,' Joan touched Jeff's arm gently. 'You should call your son, explain everything to him.'

Jeff sighed, 'I'd like to, I suppose I've just felt so bad about my behaviour, and his mother pretty much banned me from seeing him.'

'Oh, the poor little thing has fallen asleep under the table,' Joan reached down and picked up the puppy, cradling it as it nuzzled against her sleepily. 'We should give it some more food.'

The puppy ate from its bowl enthusiastically before lapping some water and running off into the lounge, where it jumped up onto the sofa and nestled down between Mary and Archie, waking Mary, who stroked it as she looked up in surprise.

'Matthew, you little horror, take that tinsel off of poor Dulcie right now,' she reached up, laughing, to her own head, where strands of silver tree decorations had been draped over her hair.

Skipping Christmas in Holly Crescent

The lounge, and its sleeping occupants, had been transformed into a Christmas grotto, with Archie and Andrew as sleeping Santa Clauses in their red Santa hats.

As Matthew's laughter woke everyone up, Michaela took photos of the spectacle and before long they were all laughing along with him.

'I should get the oven on,' Mary stood up, realising the time.

'I'll look after this little chap, keep him out of the way,' Archie settled the puppy on his knees.

'Can we play some Christmas music?' Matthew looked hopefully at his grandparents, 'it's not like Christmas otherwise.'

Archie winked at Mary, who gave him a small shrug and a nod. 'Why not? I think you'll find a couple of Christmas CDs somewhere in the cupboard there.

'CDs? We don't need those, I'll use my phone,' Matthew tapped his screen and Mariah Carey's voice sang out, with Matthew accompanying her, his voice yelling out tunelessly, 'All I want for Christmas is you', just as Jeff and Joan walked into the lounge. Jeff smiled at Joan and she felt herself blush a little.

Archie smiled down at the puppy on his lap as he hummed along, and Mary felt a warm glow inside. Her idea would work, she was sure of it.

Tracy carried some of the books into the lounge, asking Archie if he minded her sharing some photos on social media.

'I've no idea what that is, and I think I'm too old to need to know,' he smiled fondly at her, 'but if it means that other people get to see these wonderful old treasures, then please go ahead, share away. And, Tracy, I meant what I said about taking some of these, we don't need them, don't have the space for them, so you are welcome to help yourself, love.'

'Thanks,' Tracy flushed with pleasure as she gently touched the books, 'I'll just borrow some, if that's okay, they're far too valuable for me to keep them.'

Mary inserted herself into the conversation, 'I think that sounds fine, and it means we'll get to see plenty of you when you come to return books and collect different ones. We could make it a kind of regular thing if you like, and you could have a spot of dinner with us, maybe make it a bit of a book evening. How does that sound?'

Michaela looked up at Nigel as they laid the books they'd brought down, on the coffee table, to find him looking at her, and they both blushed and looked away.

'Like a book club but for old books?' Tracy's face lit up, 'I love the sound of that.'

'Me too, Michaela surprised everyone, 'I could come over, couldn't I, Mum?'

Susan's eyebrows rose to her hairline, 'Of course, darling.'

'And, Nigel, you could come, if you wanted to...'

'I'll definitely join you,' he nodded enthusiastically.

'Well, that's settled then, we'll start our own book club.'

'It'll need a name.'

Mary left them to their excited chattering. 'Right, it's time to get organised for dinner, who wants to help?' Her call to action brought eager offers from everyone and she began to give instructions as everyone bustled around.

With the oven nice and hot, Mary slid the glazed gammon in on the top shelf, before preparing trays for the other food.

His battery must be flat, that was just perfect. Slamming the car door closed, Richard ordered a taxi, stamping his feet against the cold that seeped into his feet and through his body. Twenty minutes to wait for the taxi, he sighed, unlocking his front door again, he'd have to wait indoors if he didn't want to turn into a block of ice.

The table was transformed into a festive display, albeit a vulgar one, as Matthew liberally draped tinsel between the placemats and placed coloured baubles in every available gap, singing along tunelessly to the Band Aid song as it played out into the room.

'I'm sorry about all this, Dulcie,' Mary turned from the sideboard, a pile of mismatched napkins in her hands, 'it seems to have descended into chaos.'

Dulcie's face broke into a big smile as she looked around at the scene, 'It's absolutely wonderful, just what Andrew and I needed. Here, give me those napkins. Andrew,' she called her husband, 'come and help me with these.'

Delicious aromas began to come from the oven as the chicken pie warmed, and soon the appetizing aroma of pizzas, chips, and sausages had everyone feeling hungry.

'Would you take these through, Susan? I expect everyone would like a sausage roll while they wait.'

'Let's crack open these boxes of wine,' Andrew suggested to Archie, who agreed enthusiastically. 'Where are the glasses?'

'I'll get them if you point me in the right direction,' Jeff offered as he munched on a sausage roll.

Tracy finished posting her photos of the books to her Instagram account and put her phone in her back pocket, before bringing Mary a glass of wine, her face flushed with eagerness, 'Did you have any ideas about the puppy?' she asked anxiously.

'I did, I'm going to speak to Archie and see what he thinks about us keeping him, but if I'm right, he's coming to the idea all on his own. Now, I need someone to slice the ham, who's free?'

'Shall I do it?' Jeff took charge and expertly carved up the gammon.

Michaela studied the dinner table - it was probably just about the worst decorated Christmas dinner table that she'd ever seen, but it was also kind of magical and fun. She took photos as Helen ferried the dishes of food through, squeezing them in wherever there was space, and finished up with a group shot after setting her phone onto its timer. Everyone cheered and clapped for the photo, before turning their attention to the meal.

Matthew was tasked with refilling glasses and in between mouthfuls he removed people's glasses, filling them almost to the brim in his excitement at the whole thing.

'I forgot the crackers,' Joan whispered to Jeff.

'I'll get them. Nigel,' he beckoned Joan's son, 'I need your help with something.'

More cheers erupted when the crackers were handed out and George Michael's Last Christmas was momentarily drowned out by the sound of ripping paper and loud cracks as they were pulled apart. Multi-coloured paper hats were placed on heads, jokes read out, and trinkets examined, before more food was appreciatively consumed.

'Did anyone hear something?' Susan cocked her head, 'I thought I heard a knocking sound.'

They fell silent for a moment, just as Chris Rea began Driving home for Christmas.

'There it is again, I think there's someone at the door.'

'I'll go,' Archie stood up, his face flushed from the wine.

'Hello, Dad,' Richard stepped inside, grinning at his father's bewildered expression. 'Surprise. I thought you and Mum might like a bit of company, can't have you sitting all alone on Christmas Day. Oh-' Suddenly he became aware of the chatter and laughter coming from the dinner table, the music playing, and the puppy, who'd accompanied Archie to the front door.

'You've got company. And a dog.' he stated the obvious, feeling nonplussed for a second.

'Who is it, love?' Mary walked out of the lounge door, stopping in surprise at the sight of her son. 'Richard! Why aren't you in Thailand?'

'It's a long story. Happy Christmas, Mum, Dad, I picked up these on the way,' he held out the sorry-looking flowers and the box of chocolates he'd found at a petrol station which the taxi driver had kindly stopped at for him, on the way. 'And I brought a bottle of wine,' he held that out too.

'They're beautiful, thank you, Richie, now give your mum a hug,' Mary held out her arms as Archie thanked him for the wine and took the bottle from him.

'Oh, Mum, I'm sorry I've been such a useless son. Dad,' Richard pulled his father into the embrace, 'I should have called you from Thailand, I should have let you know I was there safely. But more than that, I should have been in touch more, I should have visited, and I should have wished you both a Happy Christmas. I've been a terrible son, but I want to make up for it.'

Mary and Archie raised their eyebrows at each other behind their son's back and Archie stepped back, looking at him in concern. 'You're not going to burst into tears are you, son?'

'You've got nothing to apologise for, we know you've got your own life, you and Sandy have probably just been busy, we know how it is when you're younger,' Mary hastened to reassure him.

'Richard, Mum and Dad said you were in Thailand,' Helen appeared, munching on a pig in blanket, her yellow hat lopsided on her head.

'Hi, Hels, what are you doing here? I thought you'd be at some party with all your arty friends.'

'Suze,' Helen yelled, 'guess who's here?'

'Susan's here as well?

Matthew raced into the hall, skidding to a halt as his hat fell off. 'Hi, Uncle Richard, d'you want some pizza?'

'Pizza?' Richard's face was baffled.

Skipping Christmas in Holly Crescent

Mary laughed, 'Come through, I'll introduce you to everyone, and then you can have some pizza and chips.'

Richard shook his head in confusion, his dreams of a roast turkey dinner dissipating in front of his eyes.

'Let me take your bag,' Archie picked up the bag from where Richard had dropped it in his surprise, 'I'm afraid if you were thinking of staying there's no room at the inn, son, we're a little full to say the least.'

'Everyone, meet Richard, our son,' Mary clapped her hands delightedly as she made introductions, and Jeff fetched another chair from the kitchen.

Tracy's phone dinged a few times in rapid succession and she looked up apologetically before excusing herself from the table to step away and see what all the notifications were about.

Michaela's and Nigel's phones did the same thing and they excused themselves too, the three of them standing huddled with their eyes glued to their screens.

'Who's Bibliophil?' Michaela looked at Tracy's happy face.

'That's Phil, from work, it's his play on words, like, Bibliophile – for book lover – and leaving the 'e' off so that it includes his name,' Tracy laughed delightedly at the cleverness of her colleague, as Michaela made deductions.

'He seems to like a lot of your posts, and, oh, look, here's another comment he's just left.'

Nigel grinned as she nudged him, the two of them watching Tracy's pink face as she read the new comment.

A little while later, Richard sat back, replete from his strange meal of chicken pie and slices of gammon, pizza and chips, and a side of pigs in blankets. 'And that's that, I just crept out of the room and took a taxi to the airport, and here I am.'

Helen burst out laughing, 'I can't believe you left your wife sleeping in a hotel room in Thailand. That's got to be the funniest story I've heard in a long time.'

'I do feel a little guilty, but–'

'She was cheating on you, she deserved it,' Susan's face dropped for a moment as she thought of Trevor. What a sorry state they were, she and her brother.

'This food was actually delicious,' Richard grinned, 'weird, unexpected, but absolutely delicious. Now, is someone going to tell me who this little puppy belongs to?'

Mary looked at Archie, maybe now was the time to make a gentle suggestion. She winked at Tracy, who smiled hopefully.

'Well, Tracy was fostering him, weren't you, dear? But Tracy's landlord has told her the puppy has to go, poor little thing...' she glanced at Archie.

'What? What sort of an excuse for a human being behaves like that?' Archie picked up the puppy, cuddling him on his knees, 'He should stay with us. Would you like that? You would?' He tilted the puppy's head up as he spoke to him, stroking him under his chin, and looking across at Mary to ask, 'What d'you think? Poor little thing needs a home.'

'And he'll get plenty of love, which he'll give us in equal quantities,' she smiled at her husband, 'I think it's a wonderful idea, Archie, you're awfully clever and kind to have come up with it.' She winked triumphantly at Tracy as Archie grinned, his eyes twinkling.

'D'you two think I didn't know what you were up to? I've been onto to you for a while now, since I saw you huddled together earlier.'

'Oh, Archie, you rotter,' Mary tapped his arm playfully, as Tracy beamed with relief. 'And Tracy, you'll visit him often, I hope?'

Tracy's beam grew even wider, 'I'd love to.'

'So, are we keeping him? Promise?' Matthew grinned and clapped his hands.

'We are, love.'

'We must give him a name,' Michaela took the puppy from her grandad, holding him close. 'And he'll need lots of walks, you and grandad might get a bit tired...' she glanced towards Nigel.

'We could walk him sometimes, all of us, I mean, Matthew, Tracy, you, and me,' he felt his cheeks burn and ran his fingers through his hair to hide his embarrassment.

Susan looked from her daughter to Nigel, in surprise, there was a budding romance playing out right under her nose. The thought made her happy, and then sad, as she thought of the demise of her own romance with Trevor.

As if reading her mind, Matthew asked, 'I wish Trevor was here, when's he coming?'

Mary intervened, 'What shall we call this little darling? Who's got a suggestion?'

'Christmas.'

Everyone looked at Matthew as they slowly began to nod. It would make a lovely name.

'Then every time we call his name, we'll remember this Christmas that we all spent together, the best Christmas ever. Mum, can we have pizza for Christmas next year?' He looked at his mum hopefully as laughter rang out from around the table, unaware of the wonderful sentiment he'd just expressed.

'I think Christmas is the perfect name, love. What do you think, Christmas?' Mary smiled lovingly at the puppy still cradled in Michaela's arms, who wriggled his answer happily.

'He loves it, let's take Christmas outside,' Matt leapt up as a knock sounded on the front door.

Mary did a mental count on her fingers, she had three children, all of whom had arrived unexpectedly, so that just left...

'Trevor!' Susan exclaimed in surprise as Archie showed him into the lounge, 'what are you doing here?' She didn't know what to make of his appearance and, red-faced, she turned to the table, 'Mum, Dad, everyone, this is Trevor, my, er-' Was he still her boyfriend? What should she call him?

'Susan's boyfriend,' he smiled around the table. 'It's very nice to meet you all, and especially the two of you, Mr and Mrs Nugent.'

'Please call us Mary and Archie, Trevor. It's lovely to meet you finally.'

He looked at Susan, his face drawn, 'At least, I hope I'm still your boyfriend? Am I?'

Susan's eyes filled with tears as her heart thudded, happiness growing inside. He still wanted to be with her. 'You are,' she whispered.

Oblivious to the drama playing out in front of everyone, Matthew flung his arms around Trevor, 'You missed the best ever Christmas dinner, and Bagatelle, and everything, and we've all adopted a puppy together.'

'What?' Trevor laughed, his eyes still on Susan as he hugged Matthew.

'Well, Grandma and Grandad have adopted him, and we're calling him Christmas, but we're all going to take him for walks, so we're sharing him. That's right, isn't it, Grandma?'

'I couldn't have put it better myself. Now, why don't you kids take Christmas out into the garden for a bit, but put your coats on, it looks freezing outside. Don't let Christmas get too cold, alright?' She stood up, touching Susan's shoulder, 'Why don't you and Trevor go up to our room and have a chat? And then, if you're hungry, I'll put a plate of food together for you, Trevor.'

'Thanks, Mary, that sounds great,' Trevor smiled his thanks at her, before reaching for Susan's hand.

Trevor closed the bedroom door, taking Susan in his arms and burying his face in her hair as she sobbed.

'I'm sorry, I've ruined everything for you, I made a fool of myself and made you a laughing stock.'

'No, I'm sorry, love, it was my fault, I should have told you what was going on.'

'I know you cheated on me, but I don't blame you, and I don't blame you for leaving me, I'm fat and-'

'Cheated on you?' Trevor stood back to gaze into Susan's eyes in confusion, 'I haven't cheated on you, whatever gave you that idea?'

'You didn't? But what about Pam?' Wiping her eyes, Susan grabbed a tissue from the box beside the bed.

'Pam? That nasty piece of work? And you can add Ronnie, Dickson's vacuous, vindictive, girlfriend to the list, and the whole lot of them, if you ask me. Well, apart from Sybil, the one decent person in the whole company.'

Hope began to flutter inside her as his words registered. 'Sybil is nice,' she nodded, 'it's a shame she's retiring.'

'Let's sit down, I want to show you something, and then I'll explain.'

Trevor held out his phone to show Susan the photo of her ignominious entrance through the curtains onto the runway, as she grimaced in shame.

'Don't, I can't bear to look at it.'

'Wait,' he enlarged the photo, zooming in on the background. 'See?'

Susan took his phone, peering at the image of Ronnie, an evil grin on her face as her hand clearly shoved Susan's back. Pam stood beside her, laughing with a cruel glint in her eyes. 'That's why I fell over,' she whispered.

'Well, that and the fact that you'd had a bit too much to drink,' Trevor grinned at her, 'and hadn't eaten anything. Sybil phoned me this morning, after she saw the photos, and told me that she'd overhead Ronnie laughing about it with a bunch of them, including Pam. Both Pam and Ronnie knew you hadn't eaten anything and were sloshed, but they encouraged you to go ahead because they thought it would be funny. Sybil heard Ronnie say, 'that'll teach her for attracting the attention of my boyfriend, showing off her huge bosom, as if Dickson could seriously ever like that.' She was jealous, Suze, she'd overhead Dickson's inappropriate comment when we arrived and she wanted revenge.'

Skipping Christmas in Holly Crescent

'Ronnie was jealous of me?'

'Why are you so surprised? I mean, look at her, the woman's a walking stick insect. But you? You're gorgeous.'

Susan's face brightened, a small smile beginning to form even as her eyes remained anxious, 'But, what about Pam? You were spending the whole time, at both parties, trying to impress her, you were chasing her around and I felt so stupid.'

'Have you noticed the average age of everyone else at work? I'm practically old enough to be the father of any one of them, apart from good old Sybil. My own boss is practically a child. I was losing ground, struggling to stay in the game while they all brought in the new contracts. Pam's my supervisor and was directed by Dickson to make some staff cuts. I've spent the last few weeks desperately trying to hold onto my job.'

'I wish you'd told me, love, I could have tried to help instead of making everything harder for you.'

'I should have, but I didn't want to worry you. After Sybil's call this morning, I made a decision. I went to Dickson's and resigned, being sure to tell him what an absolute treasure his girlfriend was, and what a nasty blot Pam was on the face of the business. I called in at my parents' and explained that we couldn't make it today and that we'd rearrange, and then I went to the office and left huge photocopies of Ronnie pushing you over while Pam watched, laughing. Don't worry,' he hastened to reassure Susan, 'I blurred you out. And' he smiled grimly, clearly pleased with himself, 'I added horns to both of their heads. It was a nice touch, I think. There's one stuck to every person's screen for when they get into work. I also posted the pictures to the company's facebook page for good measure.'

Susan grinned, her misery lifting, apart from one remaining worry, 'But now you don't have a job?'

'Well, that's the funny and amazing thing about social media. A couple of people have reached out to me after seeing my post and I've got meetings next week.' He held Susan's arms as he looked lovingly into her eyes, 'So everything's going to be alright.'

She winced as his grip touched her rash.

'What is it? What's wrong? Are you in pain?'

'Promise not to laugh when I tell you?' At his nod, she asked, 'But first, could you put some calamine lotion on for me?'

As she put her top back on, Trevor shook his head, laughing gently at her sorry tale of the air freshener. 'That's my fault as well, rushing you to get ready, in my panic.' He held her, kissing her softly, 'So are we alright?'

'Yes,' Susan snuggled against him happily.

'Then, do you think I could take your mum up on the offer of some food? I'm absolutely starving.'

They walked back downstairs as Andrew and Dulcie were saying their goodbyes.

'We've had the most marvellous Christmas with you all and we can't thank you enough.'

A commotion ensued as Christmas and his loyal devotees rushed back in, their faces flushed from the cold, and the elderly couple petted Christmas, before saying goodbye to the younger ones. Mary promised to bring them round some of the leftover food the following day, handing them some hurriedly wrapped Christmas cake to take with them, which they'd completely forgotten about, and Jeff informed them that he'd bring their table and chairs back in the morning, if they were happy about that, which they were.

They walked next door to their home and walked into the quiet. 'That's got to have been one of the best Christmas Days we've ever had,' Dulcie smiled, 'with some of the best people. And the strangest meal ever, but delicious,' she laughed, 'Alasdair and Gwyneth will laugh when I tell them.'

'Tell you what, I'll put the kettle on. Why don't you give them a call and tell them all about it?' Andrew smiled at his wife, humming as he headed for the kitchen.

Mary placed a plate of hot food in front of Trevor, who attacked it ravenously, looking enquiringly at her daughter, who nodded and smiled at her, looking radiant, to Mary's relief.

Archie looked across at Jeff, noting the man's slightly distracted look, 'Penny for them, Jeff.'

'What's that? Oh, sorry I was miles away,' Jeff smiled apologetically. 'Thinking about the future, I suppose, trying to work out what I'm going to do.'

'You can stay here as long as you like, can't he, Mary?'

'You certainly can,' she beamed, 'You feel like part of the family now, so no worrying, you take your time and find your feet.'

Nigel nudged Joan, whispering urgently at her, 'Tell him, Mum.'

Joan looked embarrassed as everyone waited for her to speak.

43

Linzi Carlisle

'It's just, well, Nigel had an idea, it's not perfect, far from it in fact, quite terrible if I'm honest, but it's above the shop and-'

Nigel could stand his mum's prevaricating no further, 'There's an empty flat above Mum's shop and we think you should move in. I'll help you clear it out, it's a bit full of boxes and stuff.'

'So will I,' Matthew joined in gleefully.

'Me too,' Michaela squealed excitedly, as Tracy offered to help as well.

Jeff looked at Joan in astonishment as she blushed, cursing her face's betrayal.

'It's an awful flat, I've just used it for storage, and it needs decorating, but it's got a bedroom and a bathroom.'

'And a lounge with a little kitchen.'

'Well, a kitchenette, it's very small.

'That's Mum's way of trying to get you to say yes,' Nigel grinned.

'But,' Jeff held out his hands, 'how could I-? I couldn't pay you, at least not at the moment. It sounds great, perfect actually, but I can't take charity, it just wouldn't be right.'

'You could help out in the shop, Mum's been saying for ages that she needs help but she can't afford it, you could help in exchange for the flat.'

Michaela, Nigel, and Tracy, high-fived each other, their plan was going to work.

'You have to say yes,' Nigel looked at him hopefully, 'tell him, Mum.'

Joan laughed, 'I think you have to do as the kids say, that's if you'd like to...'

'I've got some spare furniture you can have,' Richard piped up, 'too many rooms in my stupid house, I think I'll move to somewhere smaller, maybe a bit closer to here. I can't afford the house anyway, thanks to my soon-to-be ex-wife and her spendthrift ways.'

'I could help decorate, I'm a dab hand at painting stage scenery, it's the only work I get these days, and there's loads of discarded paint laying around that's just going to waste,' Helen offered her services as Joan smiled at her gratefully.

'You're actually very artistic, Helen,' Mary smiled proudly, 'your talents are wasted on the stage, you should be one of those interior designers, or whatever they call themselves.'

'An interior decorator,' mused Helen, it was an interesting idea... actually, it was a fabulous idea, she thought excitedly. Maybe it was time for a career move...

'Well?' Matthew looked at Jeff impatiently.

Jeff's face broke into an enormous grin, 'Yes, thank you. I'd love to accept.' He and Joan shared a smile as her heart did a little flutter.

'You should call your son,' Mary quietly suggested to Jeff as cheers erupted, 'Tell him your good news. There's a phone upstairs if you'd like to.'

'You're the second person to suggest that to me today,' Jeff smiled at Mary and then Joan. 'He might not want to talk to me though,' he said doubtfully.

'Or, a call from his dad might make his day...'

'There's only one way to find out, but you must make the call when the time feels right.'

Trevor wiped his mouth on the napkin, 'That was perfect, Mary, thank you. Arriving at your home unannounced, never having met you, and being fed by you, on Christmas Day, wasn't exactly the way I'd planned being introduced to Susan's parents, but today seems to just be one of those days.'

'A day of unexpected happenings,' Susan sat close to him, her hand on his arm, as Mary removed his empty plate.

A Christmas cracker was stuck under Trevor's nose. 'You have to pull a cracker,' announced Matthew, 'it's not Christmas Day if you don't.' He held one end and waited expectantly.

'You're right,' Trevor grinned, taking hold of the other end of the cracker 'no cheating now.'

The cracker pulled apart with a bang, a folded hat and a plastic trinket landing on the table in front of Trevor.

'What did you get?' asked Matthew eagerly, 'I got a measuring tape, and Michaela got a keyring.'

Trevor picked up the bright green object, holding it in his hand as he turned to Susan. Moving his chair back, he bent down on one knee as the room fell silent.

'Susan Chavers, I love you and I want to be with you for the rest of our lives. Will you marry me?' His eyes looked directly into hers as she clasped her chest, taking a deep breath.

'Yes,' she gasped happily, her eyes filling with tears.

'Now that's the kind of crying I like to see,' Archie grinned in approval, 'tears of happiness.'

44

Skipping Christmas in Holly Crescent

Hooting and clapping drowned out the words Trevor and Susan were whispering to each other, which was just as well, as they were private, and meant only for each other's ears.

Mary hugged Archie, before hugging Susan and Trevor, followed by every other person in the room, finishing with Christmas, who snuggled against her, unaware of the momentous event which had just occurred.

Michaela took photo after photo. It would ruin her Instagram theme but she didn't care. It would be filled with memories of the absolute best day of her life, she thought happily, smiling prettily at Nigel.

'Well, at least one of us is going to be happily married,' Richard grinned ruefully. 'Congratulations, sis, and to you, Trevor.' He looked at his watch, 'I should be getting home, leave you chaps to it. I expect there'll be some suitably soppy film on the television tonight to keep me company as I get used to my new single state. I'm really happy for you both,' he shook Trevor's hand before pulling his sister into a bear hug, 'be happy, sis, you deserve it. And make sure he gets you a real ring, that green plastic thing is hideous,' he winked at his sister as they all laughed.

'Oh, I don't know, I quite like it,' she laughed. 'Thanks, Rich,' Susan smiled, her heart overflowing with happiness as she looked around her.

'I won't have to be a page boy or anything, will I?' Matthew screwed up his face as his mum clung tightly to his hand.

'Oh, I don't know, you might look kind of cute in a little red velvet suit with, what d'you reckon,' Trevor winked at Susan, 'a flowery bowtie?'

'No way,' Matthew groaned, doubling over in laughter, 'not unless Micky has to wear a disgusting flowery bridesmaid's dress.'

'I will, just to see you dressed up,' she teased.

'I'll share a taxi with you if you like?' Helen hugged her brother, I ought to be getting home.'

'I've got a spare room, fancy keeping your old brother company? We could do the sibling thing, it's been a while, and I promise to supply you with tissues if we watch a soppy film.'

'Yes, why not?' Helen grinned, it'll be better than going back to my flat and waiting for Bianca to get in and regale with me with stories of who was lunching at Salvatore's today.'

Richard turned to his parents, hugging them both fiercely, 'Being here today has been really nice, thanks for letting me barge in and join you all. It's reminded me of how important family is, and of how good it is for the soul to just be together, laughing and having fun, with good people.'

'I couldn't have put it better myself,' Helen kissed her mum and dad, hugging them closely for a second, 'thank you, both of you, for always being here for us all.'

Jeff walked back down the stairs, his face shining with an extra little glow of happiness, unnoticed by anyone except Joan, who caught his eye. Sharing a private smile with her, Jeff turned to join in with the goodbyes underway.

'Right, let's go, bye everyone,' Helen shoved her brother out of the door, giving them all one last wave as they stood in the doorway, her chattering voice carrying in the still of the evening.

'You design websites don't you, Rich? You could make me one for my new interior decorator business.'

'You'll have to pay me, I don't have any money left.'

'Sure, when I'm rich and famous.'

Archie closed the door on the laughing siblings, turning to his wife, 'Quite the turn of events today.'

'It's been a day full of surprises,' Mary's face shone as the music was turned up in the living room and Shakin' Stevens joined the party. She looked around at the untidy room, feeling a surge of pleasure. To think that she'd convinced herself that a tidy lounge with no mess to clean up had seemed like a nice idea only a day or two ago. This was how it should be, she nodded to herself, all the untidiness told its own happy story of a day enjoyed by everyone.

Matthew sang along loudly, with the others joining in here and there. 'Snow is falling.'

'All around me.'

'I wish it was snowing,' Matthew yelled as he danced around the room.

Jeff looked out of the window, beckoning Matthew, as he grinned.

They all sang the last line together, 'Merry Christmas Everyone,' as they gathered around the window, gazing at the first few snowflakes as they drifted gently down.

'Can we stay tonight, Mum?' Matthew looked pleadingly at Susan, 'Please?'

She and Trevor exchanged a glance, 'I don't see why not, Trevor and I could have a quiet evening together.'

Trevor squeezed her shoulders as he pulled her close, 'That sounds perfect. We'll come and get you tomorrow.'

Susan and Trevor left amidst much hugging and laughter and Joan looked regretfully at her watch.

'I suppose we ought to be getting home, Nige, I've got to be up to open the shop tomorrow.'

'I'll walk you home, Jeff offered, much to her pleasure.

'I should leave too,' Tracy spoke as her phone dinged and she read the message, her face turning a delicate shade of pink.

'Is it him?' Michaela looked at her knowingly, 'What did he say?'

'He asked me what I'm doing tomorrow,' she said shyly to the interested faces watching her.

'Tracy's got a boyfriend,' Matthew teased her.

'Tell him to meet us at the shop, we can all help Jeff to start clearing out the boxes from the flat,' Michaela looked at Joan, 'that is, if it's alright?'

'That sounds great, the more the merrier,' Joan smiled, Boxing Day was looking a lot more fun than she'd expected it to be.

'Thank you for the most perfect day,' Tracy hugged Mary and Archie, before picking up Christmas for a cuddle. 'I'll see you soon,' she whispered to the puppy.

'And we'll see you soon for our first book club,' Mary said.

'Old Friends,' Nigel said suddenly 'that's what we should call it, The Old Friends Book Club.'

'Perfect,' Michaela clapped.

'It really is, you clever thing,' Mary gave her seal of approval, 'old books are like old friends, and although we're all new friends, something tells me we'll be old friends soon enough.'

'If you're sure that it's alright to start on the flat tomorrow, then I might ask Luke to join us,' Jeff looked enquiringly at Joan as she beamed.

'And then we can all come back here and I can show Luke how to play Bagatelle, and Grandma can make us sandwiches and we can have leftover pizza.'

They all laughed at Matthew's one-track mind as they gathered their coats and jackets.

'It's truly been a day to remember, thank you,' Joan hugged her hosts warmly.

Jeff and Joan walked along the road to the flats, laughing at Matthew's non-stop chatter, snowflakes landing on their hair.

Tracy waved goodbye with promises to see them all in the morning, entering her flat and throwing herself down on her old sofa as she replayed the events of the day in her mind, hugging herself in happiness as she read Phil's message saying that he'd love to help tomorrow.

They stopped outside Joan's flat, suddenly the only two people in the world, and Jeff brushed a snowflake from Joan's nose as they laughed, before falling silent.

'Happy Christmas, Joan,' Jeff's eyes looked into hers lovingly.

'Happy Christmas, Jeff,' Joan smiled shyly.

'What were the rest of those lyrics from the song that Matthew was just playing?' murmured Jeff, 'I'm gonna find that girl?'

'Underneath the mistletoe,' Joan whispered.

'We'll kiss by candlelight...'

Joan allowed herself to be pulled gently into his embrace as their lips touched.

Michaela glanced from under her hair at Nigel as they hovered together, 'It's been a really great day, hasn't it?'

'It's been perfect,' Nigel hugged her, kissing her shyly, as her stomach did a backflip. For once she forgot about taking a photo as she returned his kiss.

Matthew pranced in the snow as it began to fall heavily, oblivious to the love blossoming in the air around him. 'I've just realised, we're going to be clearing out boxes on Boxing Day,' he whooped in delight to no one in particular.

'Isn't it wonderful?' Mary held her hands out as the snowflakes landed gently in her palms before melting, 'what a perfect end to a perfect day.'

46

Skipping Christmas in Holly Crescent

'You realise that skipping Christmas turned out to be more of a real Christmas than anything we could have imagined?' Archie's eyes shone. 'We thought we could avoid all that fuss and bother, and instead we had fun, friendship, family, laughter, and plenty of enjoyable fuss and bother.'

'We had trials and tribulation, tears and laughter, and love and friendship,' Mary's voice was soft, 'and most of all, we had happy endings.'

We had Christmas after all, even if it was unintentional. And do you know what the funniest thing is?' Archie looked down at the puppy, 'We've now got Christmas every day of the year.'

Christmas gave a small bark of happiness as Mary stooped and picked him up, smothering him in kisses. 'Christmas every day, I like the sound of that, don't you, Christmas?'

Christmas licked her face as they both laughed and turned and walked back inside.

Linzi Carlisle is the author of the Sasha Blue Mystery Series. This is her first Christmas story.

She grew up in Dartford, Kent, in the UK, before moving to Africa, where she met her husband. She spent thirteen memorable years in Chingola, Zambia, and five years enjoying the wines in the Winelands of the Western Cape, before settling in the Garden Route in South Africa. She and her husband live in the beautiful town of George, nestled between the Outeniqua Mountains and the Indian Ocean. They have been the proud parents of many beloved children of the four-legged variety over the years, these being, at the time of publication, two beautiful rescue cats.

Blogger: www.linzicarlisle.blogspot.com
Instagram: @linzicarlisleauthor
Facebook: @linzicarlisleauthor
Amazon: amazon.com/author/linzicarlisle

Printed in Great Britain
by Amazon